JUDGE RANDALL
DISCOVERS
HEAVY METAL

JUDGE RANDALL DISCOVERS HEAVY METAL

TONY ROGERS

A Judge Randall Mystery

Other titles in the Judge Randall series:

ISBN: 979-8-9864655-4-8 (Paperback)
ISBN: 979-8-9864655-5-5 (Ebook)

Published by Quinn Cove Books

Thanks again to Joan Seymour for her invaluable editorial help.

Cover Design by Berge Design

To Tamara

1

Retired judge Jim Randall's routine when he woke up was much the same at Pat's apartment and his townhouse: lie on his back debating the merits of getting up, the pros and cons, judge the arguments objectively as befitting a former judge; then give in to the need to eat and get out of bed. Pat's Beacon Hill apartment was quieter in the morning than Jim's Cambridge townhouse, but both places had a city hum that usually went unnoticed because it was constant, a background hum that Jim assumed came from I-90 and I-93.

Lulled by the hum, he trekked into Pat's kitchen to pour himself coffee; the distance from Pat's bedroom to her kitchen was not great but at Jim's age (he had just turned 70 – which he still couldn't believe) early morning walks were starting to feel like treks. Pat had already gone to her pro bono work at Essex University so Jim had the kitchen to himself. Whenever he stayed at Pat's, he was tempted to ask her secret for great coffee but he liked having some unsolved mysteries in life.

He took his coffee into her living room and sat facing the windows. He liked looking out her windows although the view was across a narrow street to an unchanging wall of red brick apartments; at Jim's townhouse the view was of two and three decker houses; at his Vermont house, the view was across the ever-changing Connecticut River.

The morning's headline in the *Boston Globe* read, "**Essex Student Still Missing**." Pat's pro bono work since she retired from the bench included mentoring Essex law students, and the missing student was someone she mentored, a well-meaning young woman Pat had taken to. The student's name was Connie Hawkins. She came from an old New England family that had made its fortune in retail and now owned a chain of shopping centers. Connie's father, Drexel, was the black sheep of the Hawkins family, having squandered his inheritance on foolish schemes. Connie's older brother, Timothy, was a musician currently performing in Paris who had no interest in business. The Hawkins conglomerate now was run (badly) by Drexel's surviving brother, Edward, who wanted out. He preferred fishing off a dock at Key West, or dropping a line off the stern of his boat, *Fortitude*. Connie, being the only Hawkins descendent with a shred of business sense, was expected to redeem the family name once she earned her law degree but she wasn't sure the family business would be a good fit for her.

Jim Randall, ever practical except when struck by an occasional, disconcerting touch of whimsey, had asked Pat, "Why doesn't Connie try the family business before she makes up her mind what she wants to do with her life?"

"Because she isn't convinced shopping centers have a future. And because she's afraid of the pressures she would feel once she's in the family business," Pat had replied. "She thinks she would feel trapped."

Jim backed up. "Is that why Connie went to law school instead of business school?"

Pat answered. "I asked her a version of that question. Her answer was, yes, to avoid feeling trapped on a predetermined path. She's a good kid when she lets down her guard, but she's one of the most guarded people I've ever met."

"Which leads to the inevitable next question: do you think her disappearance is voluntary?"

"I think that's most likely. There's no sign of foul play."

"Then why did it make the *Globe*?"

"Because of a chance to link the Hawkins name with the word 'kidnaped.'"

*

Sasha Cohen, who broke the story for the *Globe*, was a friend of Jim's from her days as a cub reporter for a Boston weekly. Jim had seen potential in her and put her in contact with the *Globe*. He and Sasha had kept in touch since.

He placed a call to her. He got her answering machine.

"Hi, this is Sasha Cohen. You have reached my phone at the *Globe*. Please leave a message. If this an urgent matter, you may call my cell at 617-057-2312, but don't use that number unless it's really urgent. Have a good day."

"Sasha, this is Jim Randall. It's about the missing Essex student. The Long Gone first thing tomorrow morning?" Jim's voice rumbled along like a road grader so the only way a listener could know when Jim was asking a question was to listen carefully for a slight uptick at the end.

The Long Gone coffeehouse near Inman Square was Jim's hangout in retirement, his de facto office, a place of contemplation and regret. A venue for fueling dreams and quashing them. He had once read that the definition of home was where 'when you have to go there, they have to take you in.' The Long Gone fit that definition. The only place he felt more comfortable was his living room.

Sasha Cohen made up in intensity what she lacked in size. When she walked into The Long Gone next morning, she moved so purposefully she left a vacuum in her wake.

"Hi," she said, breathlessly sitting down across from Jim.

Sasha leaned forward, her hands wrapped around a large takeout container of coffee. "It's funny that you called me because I was about to call you. I reached a friend of Connie's who is very worried."

"How so?"

"She thinks Connie may have wanted to vanish."

"For good?"

Sasha nodded. "Forever." She took her first sip of coffee. "Ouch! Too hot!"

"Give it time to cool down."

"I don't have time to waste."

"I'm a waste of time?"

"Don't be touchy, Jim. You know me: sometimes too busy to watch my words."

Jim shook his head. "Wow, you're really into this story, aren't you?"

"Connie intrigues me. If I had a family like hers, I would run away too."

"I can't see you running away from anything, Sasha. You'd stay and skewer your enemies in print."

"Or be kidnaped."

Jim perked up. "You think?"

"A father-daughter problem made to look like a kidnaping? Is that what I think? I don't know what to think. I was hoping you could help."

"Be glad to but Pat is closer to the subject."

"But I know how to read you and I barely know Pat. Oh, shit. I'm late. Have to run."

Before Jim could reply, Sasha levitated out the door. Jim admired Sasha and was amused by her in equal measure. The two women Jim admired most in the world were Pat and Sasha, for very different reasons. One was solid in word and manner, one was hyper, but each did her job better than anyone else.

Jim settled in for the long haul. The Long Gone cooperated. One had to rise to refill one's cup but otherwise moving was not imperative.

He gathered his thoughts, then texted Pat a brief summary of his meeting with Sasha.

She called in reply. "Sounds intriguing. I want to hear more. Can it wait until tonight?"

"Absolutely. By then, it will be embellished beyond recognition, but absolutely, it can wait."

"You embellisher, you. That's what I love about you. Never satisfied just to state the facts."

"Bullshit and poppycock."

"See you tonight, Jim."

Jim stood. A walk on Beauty Shop Row seemed like the thing to do at a moment like this, or at any moment, as a matter of fact. A half-dozen blocks of bustling Cambridge

Street that held more beauty and barber shops than Jim had ever imagined let alone seen. His favorite was the pink-hued facade of Rosie's House of Beauty, where he had once barely missed being felled by a furious woman barreling out the door. Who would think the memory of almost being knocked off one's feet could elicit a smile?

Walking home via Beauty Shop Row took him out of his way, but he had time to kill. No pressing duties waited for him at home. His living room was cool and dark at that hour. It got little natural light until late afternoon, so until then Jim preferred his study on the third floor. He could still make it up the stairs, but his legs felt heavier than ever and he sighed in relief as he sank into his reading chair.

Out the window, above his writing desk, he could glimpse the geometrical rooftops of Cambridge.

*

Until she vanished, Connie Hawkins lived just north of the Cambridge line in Arlington. Her boyfriend, Andy Taylor – a singer of tortured rock, stage name Crankshaft – lived with her off-and-on. Pat had met Andy while she was mentoring Connie. She didn't like him.

"I don't like Andy. I only met him once but I didn't like him," is how she put it to Jim that evening when they debriefed at his townhouse. "He's in training to cause trouble. I don't know why Connie puts up with him. He's like a bee who has gotten in the house, annoying as hell and hard to swat."

"I know the type. I used to be like that," Jim mugged.

"You used to front an angry rock band? No, you didn't."

"Okay, I didn't, but I can imagine it."

Pat gave Jim a sideways look. "Why do you do that?"

"Do what?"

"Try identities on for size."

"To see what it feels like. There's no harm as long as I know I'm doing it. It's a useful tool for an amateur detective."

"You did it before, when we were judges."

"It's an *essential* tool for a judge. Connie Hawkins – abducted or runaway? What's your guess?"

Pat answered only after careful consideration. "I got to know her well, and the more I think about her disappearance, the more I think it was voluntary. I think when she looked ahead in life she saw no way she could pursue her dreams within the family. She confided in me as her mentor that her father invested all his failed dreams in her, and she felt there was no way she could fulfill both his dreams and hers. Her dilemma is that she doesn't want to disappoint him *or* abandon her dreams." She paused for further reflection. "So she flees with a boyfriend named Crankshaft."

Jim gave a slight smile.

"Why are you smiling?"

"I'm not."

"Yes, you are. There! Why are you smiling?"

"I guess hearing a formidable woman like you say a word like Crankshaft. Say it again."

"Stop it."

"Please!" Jim pleaded.

"Stop it, Jim." Pat put the last dish in the dishwasher. "Connie's father wants to meet with me. He's worried about his daughter."

"Have you met him before?"

"Once. Early in Connie's time at the law school. He averted his eyes the whole time. I am torn between wanting to help and wanting to stay out of what I think has the potential to become a very messy situation. What should I do, Jim?"

"I think you have to meet with him for your own peace of mind. How long have you been Connie's mentor?"

"The whole time she's been at law school. I became her de facto shrink as well as her mentor."

"Remind me what she's like."

"Brainy, studious, ebullient up to the point where she thinks she might have overstepped her boundaries, then snaps shut like a turtle. She's one of the best young people I know, but she drives me crazy sometimes. *Drove* me crazy. Past tense." She paused. "I hope she's okay."

2

It was Jim's turn to stay at Pat's on Beacon Hill. The Brahmin Bistro at the base of the hill was their go-to Beacon Hill restaurant but it didn't replace Duck, Duck, Goose near Jim's townhouse.

"I have to watch my step walking downhill," Jim said, walking downhill.

"I know."

"I've told you before?"

"A thousand times."

"A thousand times?"

"Okay, hundreds. The point is, I know you, Jim, in spite of the fact you like to think of yourself as deeply hidden."

The sidewalks on Beacon Hill were as treacherous as the sidewalks of Cambridge: uneven red brick, guaranteed to trip the careless. Jim carefully watched his feet as he walked. A hardship because the Charles River could be glimpsed between the row houses when he dared look up.

Jim took Pat's hand. She glanced at him with surprise.

"Why do you look surprised? I'm an affectionate man."

"Who are we talking about?"

"Seriously. I don't squander my affection but I show it."

Pat laughed. "You certainly don't squander it."

"You are a very demanding woman. Okay, so I took your hand to keep from falling. Better?"

The bistro had plenty of empty tables that early in the evening. Jim and Pat had their pick. They chose a table by the window looking over busy Charles Street. Jim ordered Côtes du Rhône, Pat ordered a Kir Royale.

When the drinks arrived, they toasted each other.

Pat's toast: "To my squandering sweetheart."

Jim's toast: "To my demanding lover."

They touched glasses, then Pat grew serious. "I met with Connie's friend Melissa today. She's very worried. The last time she and Connie talked, Connie gave no hint that she was about to vanish. Melissa suspects Andy had something to do with it."

"Andy, i.e., Crankshaft?

"Correct. Melissa thinks Andy and Connie may have fled to start a life together free of the Hawkins family legacy. She is counting on Connie contacting her once she and Andy settle down wherever they're going."

"Or, Andy is a psychopath and is holding her captive in a basement. His stage persona is billed as evil incarnate and he may have grown too comfortable with the role. I wouldn't put anything past him."

"That's a little extreme. Connie's with Andy, I'm quite sure, but the circumstances are unclear to me." Pat was a shrewd judge of people but she relied on experience and observation, not intuition, unlike Jim who was Mr. Gut Feeling.

Jim observed, "Today's life lesson: aging is a process of learning how to walk on uneven sidewalks without tripping."

Without looking up from her menu, Pat replied, "If you say so."

"Ready to order?" the waiter said over Pat's shoulder.

While they waited for their food, Pat said, "Connie's father, Drexel Hawkins, called me today hoping I'd know why his daughter disappeared or where she was. He seemed quite upset. I had to tell him I didn't know."

"What kind of man is he?"

"Self-made, you know the type: impatient, supremely self-confident but secretly scared he'll be exposed as an imposter. His concern about Connie is genuine, however."

"Does he have any clue about what happened to her?"

"The short answer is no. He's the kind of man who leaps to conclusions and gets irritated if anyone dares challenge said conclusions. But on the phone today he seemed unsure of himself, terrified he may never see his daughter again. An unnerving phone call."

"Will you keep in touch with him?"

"I don't know how deeply I want to get involved."

"Are you kidding, Pat? You're up to your neck already."

"Okay, you're right. What should I do?"

"Stay in touch with Connie's friends and her dad."

"Aye, aye, sir." A non-judicial glint appeared in Pat's eyes. "Wouldn't it be delightful if I solved Connie's disappearance before you?"

"Delightful."

*

Jim and Pat compared notes at the end of each day.

Pat: "Several classmates of Connie Hawkins describe her boyfriend, Andy/Crankshaft, as a manipulating creep. They warned Connie about him but she wouldn't listen."

Jim said, "What does a smart young woman like Connie see in a young man named Crankshaft?"

"Connie was emotionally cloistered growing up. Her father is controlling and her mother is a shadow, which trapped Connie in a catch-22. She rebelled against her father and resented her mother for not sticking up for herself. Connie's emotional education lagged far behind her intellectual education."

"Andy/Crankshaft was a way out. Okay, I can see that, but why him in particular?"

"No outsider can answer that. Connie saw something in him, that's all we know."

"I'd like to see Crankshaft perform," Jim said.

"Apparently he's scary on stage. He paints black stripes on his face, wears a black eye mask, and prowls the stage screaming."

*

Jim liked to take afternoon naps on his sofa. Napping in bed was a recipe for feeling terrible when he woke up. The sofa was better. He was napping soundly when Pat shook him awake.

"Wake up, Jim. Connie Hawkins just texted me."

"What?" Jim struggled to sit up. "What did you just say?"

"Connie Hawkins has texted me."

Wake awake now, Jim said, "What did she say?"

"She said not to worry, she's with Andy and she'll be in touch when it's safe. She begs me not to tell her parents until she does."

"Do you think the text is legit?"

"Based on my knowledge of Connie, yes, I do."

"What does she mean, she'll be in touch when it's safe?"

"Maybe she's in danger, or maybe she fears her father's wrath."

Jim was wide awake by now, pissed at himself for sleeping so soundly.

"What I'm wondering is whether Connie is acting on her own volition or whether Andy persuaded her to flee. I'll ask Ernie Farrell to find what he can about Crankshaft. This is his bailiwick."

"In the meantime, I'll reply to Connie and tell her everyone is worried about her."

"Be careful, Pat."

"I was planning to be careless."

"Sorry, poor choice of words."

Ernie and Jim met first thing the next morning at The Long Gone. Ernie Farrell never aged. He had been in his early twenties when they first met, and still looked twenty a dozen years later. Jim thought of him as a wizard of all things digital. Able to pry information from nooks and cyber crannies that Jim didn't know existed.

The Long Gone was busy but not crowded. Jim chose a corner table near the rear.

"Andy Taylor is a person of interest. He performs under the name of Crankshaft. Do your magic."

"Magic? Is that how it seems to you?"

"I was raised in the pre-computer age."

"The Antediluvian Age, you mean."

"Okay, wise guy. Will you help me?"

"Do you doubt it?"

The Long Gone was a convenient place to meet. Half-a-mile from Ernie's office, across the street from the fire station, two blocks from Beauty Shop Row.

Ernie had findings to report the next day. He was not given to preambles. "Crankshaft posts videos of himself in menacing makeup singing angry songs about betrayal and blackmail. I get the sense he's trying to hide the fact that he's a baby-faced kid from Everett. He occasionally appears on far-right Tik Tok channels, spewing rhetoric that makes my skin crawl, but I didn't find any direct threats."

"Maybe the outlaw appeal is what attracted Connie. She probably feels she is one of the very few who can see beneath the makeup, who understands he is a sensitive soul."

"I'll let you know if I find anything else, but I can't stay now. I have work waiting back at the office. Keep me informed."

"Work? You work?"

"Yes, unlike you. Bye, Jim." Ernie stood.

"Thanks, Ernie. In the meantime send me a link to Crankshaft's videos. I want to see for myself."

"You'll absolutely love him. Your kind of music." Ernie gave Jim a jaunty little wave as he walked out the door.

The link arrived when Jim was alone at home. He watched the videos in his livingroom with the shades drawn.

If Andy Taylor was trying to look Satanic behind his face paint, he failed. To Jim, he looked squishy, terrified, grotesque.

Pat walked in while Jim was watching. "Look at this, Pat."

She leaned over his shoulder. After a moment, she recoiled. "Why on earth are you watching that?"

"That's Connie Hawkins's boyfriend, Andy Taylor, aka Crankshaft. Can you believe it?"

"She ran away with *him*?"

"Apparently."

Pat leaned down again. "He looks like a psychopath."

"Correction, he's a scared young man trying to look like a psychopath."

Pat leaned closer. "What is he chanting?"

"Evil will prevail. Lock up your children...."

Pat straightened up. "Is that supposed to be an inside joke, or does he mean what he says?"

"Who knows? If Connie needed to smash the bonds of family, she picked a good hammer."

*

Research was not Jim's thing, but he knew how to Google. Connie's family didn't come over on the Mayflower, but they weren't many years behind. Connie's great-great grandfather aspired to start a business, but the opportunities in England were limited. Hence the move to the colonies where he quickly established himself in a society that rewarded people who had aspirations and a strong work ethic.

"The Hawkinses were not aristocrats," he reported to Pat after his Google excursion.

They were sitting in Jim's kitchen after a ready-to-heat meal of spaghetti and meatballs.

"I know," Pat replied. "Connie told me about her ancestors. She inherited their strong work ethic. I know her to be a hard worker. Diligent in her studies. Top grades." Pat paused. Her pause was what is sometimes called pregnant.

"Out with it. What are you thinking?" Jim asked.

"I so hope she's okay. She and I come from different backgrounds but I identify with her."

"She's a young woman with potential, you like potential." He smiled.

"Why are you smiling?"

"I'm remembering your demeanor on the bench. Your rulings showed compassion but your face never did." He held a finger to his lips. "Don't worry, your secret is safe with me."

Pat stood.

"Are you angry with me for some reason?" Jim asked.

"Why would I be? No, I'm meeting Connie's father today and I'm dreading the look on his face when I have nothing to tell him."

"See? You are a softie."

"And you're a curmudgeon."

Her report after she met with Connie's father was wrenching.

"He broke down and sobbed. I truly feel sorry for him. He's suffering."

"Has Connie tried to contact him?"

"No."

"Did you tell him she texted you?"

"She asked me not to, remember? But I told him I was sure she was okay."

"Did he believe you?"

"Probably not, but he nodded."

"Has he ever met Crankshaft?"

"No, he's totally ignorant of his daughter's private life. I don't think he knew she had a boyfriend."

"He'll have heart failure if he ever sees one of Crankshaft's videos."

3

The Ipsa Loquitur seemed especially loud this evening. Jim leaned close to Pat's ear.

"You hear the din? That's in celebration of you. They're delighted to have the renowned Judge Knowles in their midst."

Pat surveyed the crowd. "I thought Ted was supposed to meet us here."

"He said he'd be a few minutes late. He'll be here."

A minute later, longtime ADA Ted Conover walked in − tall, serious face − his stride that of a man with no time to waste but no need to impress. He surveyed the crowd looking for Jim.

Jim leaned close to Pat's ear. "Ted's surprised to see you. I can tell."

"Didn't you tell him I'd be here?"

"I did. But his memory is on time-delay." Jim straightened up. "Ted, you remember Pat Knowles, don't you?"

Ted smiled. "Of course I do. Everyone who appeared in her courtroom remembers her. How are you, Your Honor?"

"Don't you dare call me that, even in jest."

Ted smiled. "Good to see you, Pat. How's that?"

"Better. You're looking good. Fit, unlike this man I'm with."

"Jim looks in good shape to me. Although I could kick his ass. Be right back." Ted headed to the bar.

"It's good to see him," Pat said. "I always admired the way Ted balanced the legal, political and human aspects of his job."

"Ted's a good man," Jim said.

Ted rejoined them in quick minute, drink in hand. "Cheers." He took a swallow.

"We were just praising you."

"Don't let me stop you."

Jim looked at Pat. "I think we've exhausted our short list."

Ted rationed his smiles. "Fill me in on what you've learned about Connie Hawkins."

"She's okay," Pat said. "She texted me saying she was okay but not to tell her father. They have a complicated relationship."

Ted nodded. "Okay."

Pat continued, "I was Connie's law school mentor. She trusts me. I don't want to violate her trust. My impression is that Drexel Hawkins is a sincerely worried father. I don't think his worry is an act. I think her disappearance has brought home to him how much he pressured Connie in the past."

The din in the Ipsa Loquitur swelled and diminished, rose and fell, steady like city hum then crescendoing in a burst of laughter. Jim imagined a symphonic crash of cymbals whenever it crescendoed. Strange how noise that usually was distracting could – at times – be as comforting as a baby's blanket.

He liked watching Pat engaged in intense discussion. Dignity came naturally to Pat; it was untutored, unfeigned, inherent. Had he ever seen her when she was undignified? No, and it wasn't as if she were playing a role. She couldn't help herself; the D in her DNA stood for dignified. He was a lucky man to be with her – maybe he should show it more. On the other hand, they both seemed to like the relationship they had.

Ted was explaining to Pat that the DA's office would respect Connie's wish not to tell her father. "No laws have been broken so my office will stay out of it, but I expect to be kept informed."

"Of course," Pat said.

"Thanks, Ted," Jim said.

On that note, they parted. Jim and Pat walked to Pat's apartment.

"A good man," Jim commented as he and Pat mounted the backside of Beacon Hill. Except for the constant sound of traffic at the base of the hill, the streets on the hill were quiet compared to the din in Ipsa Loquitur.

"Yes, a good man," Pat seconded. "He often got on my nerves when I was a judge, but I trusted him to be fair and honest."

They entered Pat's apartment. She switched on the lights. There was an urgent voice mail waiting for Pat. Timothy, Connie's musician brother had called from France. "I just learned that my sister has vanished. Call me. Please. I'm terribly worried."

"Should I call him back now?"

Jim checked the time difference. "It's 1:30 a.m. in Paris. Wait until later in the morning."

"I met Timothy once. Connie took me to hear his band at the B-Town Lounge. Nice guy. Shy. Ethereal."

"I'm surprised he hadn't heard before now that his sister was missing."

"Timothy is estranged from most of the family. I'll text him, tell him I got the message." She thumbed her phone. "I hate these tiny keys. There, done."

Jim and Pat were reading in her living room when her phone rang. It was Timothy. She put him on speakerphone.

"Just for your information, Jim Randall, Judge Jim Randall, is listening in on this call. We served together on the court."

"Hello, Tim," Jim said.

Timothy had acquired hints of a French accent, a slight rising of tone at the end of a sentence, as if every utterance was a question. "No one over here calls me Tim. It's Timothy."

"Then Timothy it is," Jim said.

Urgently: "Where is my sister? Where is Connie? Do either of you know?"

Pat spoke with her usual calm. "I'm sorry, Timothy, we don't, but we're sure she's okay."

"She's okay?"

"That's our assumption until proven otherwise."

The phone connection was good. It was impossible to imagine an ocean between them. "You sound tentative about that," Timothy said.

Pat answered definitively. "Timothy, we have no reason to think she's not okay."

"Except for the creep she's with. I hate him. Do you know him?"

"I met him once when he stopped by the law school."

"And you don't see why I'm worried? The character he plays in his videos is exaggerated but beneath the mask and the makeup, he's Crankshaft for real."

"You know him better than I, apparently."

Timothy kept spitting invective. "And he can't sing worth shit! I'll kill him if he has harmed my sister!"

"Okay, calm down, that gets us nowhere," Pat admonished. "Will you let us know if you hear from your sister?"

"Of course. And you'll do the same?"

Pat avoided a direct answer, instead saying, "I grew very fond of Connie in the brief time I knew her."

Timothy almost screamed, "Stop speaking of her in the past tense!"

"I'm sorry, I'm truly sorry, I just meant in the brief time I've mentored her," Pat said.

Timothy calmed. "I'm sorry, forgive me. Being far away doesn't help my nerves. I'm sure you're doing everything you can."

"We are. We'll keep in touch."

Timothy's voice softened. "Thank you. So will I."

After the call ended, Pat turned to Jim. "Did I do the right thing? I wanted to tell him I had heard from his sister."

"She asked you not to. He needs to pull himself together, we're doing everything we can."

"He can't know that. And are we?"

"Maybe, maybe not. But flying off the handle doesn't help."

"If I went missing, I hope you'd fly off the handle." Pat got to her feet.

"Where are you going?"

"The bedroom."

"Are you angry with me?"

"A little for your dismissive tone, but for the moment Connie is foremost on my mind."

Jim hated himself when he let his feelings cloud his judgement. Especially when Pat knew Connie better than he did, which meant Pat had a better chance of solving Connie's disappearance than he did. Come to think of it, maybe that's why his feelings were hurt. How petty, how childish if true. Grow up, Judge Randall, he scolded, sitting on Pat's sofa. You're a bit player in this drama.

He fell asleep on the sofa. When Pat realized he hadn't come to bed, she found him curled up on the sofa, snoring even louder than usual. She gently shook his shoulder. "Jim, it's late. Come to bed."

"What?" he sputtered. "What?" When he saw who was shaking him, he shot upright. "Did Connie call you? Is she okay?"

"No, she didn't call. You fell asleep. It's 2 a.m. You need to come to bed."

Jim stumbled to his feet, his legs not sure what they were supposed to do. "I fell asleep?"

"Like the proverbial log. Come to bed." She led him by the arm.

4

Pat got some of her best ideas first thing in the morning. Jim would find her sitting up in bed, her mind sprinting as if the finish line were in sight: he could imagine her ducking her head as runners do when they cross the finish line.

"Good morning." He was reluctant to interrupt her musings.

She glanced down at Jim still lying beside her. "In my sleep I was wondering what I'd do if I had run away with a boyfriend my parents despised and I didn't want to be found but didn't want my brother and friends to be worried."

"And?" Jim said, still flat on his back.

"I think I'd adopt a new personality and give my friends a code word to use when they wanted to reach me."

"How would you get the code word to them?"

"I realized it was a batty idea as soon as I woke up."

"Wise decision."

She smiled down at him. "Get up, Jim. Rise and shine."

He struggled upright. "I was trying to find a good reason to get up when your fast-moving brain woke me."

"My brain makes noise?"

"You didn't know?"

"What does it sound like?"

"You just gave me a reason to get out of bed. To think of an answer."

"I'll help you: Pat's brain sounds like dice being shaken."

"Like an approaching freight train."

"Like fingernails on a blackboard."

Jim pulled on a pair of pants. "I'm hungry. I'll be in the kitchen when you decide to get up."

Ten minutes later, Pat joined him. "Good morning."

"About time. I've been up for ages."

She ignored that. "Has Timothy called again?"

"Do you expect him to?"

"Yes."

"Why? Tell me. My brain wakes up slower than yours."

She shook her head. "For the sake of our relationship, I shall ignore the chasm you just opened for the comeback of comebacks."

Jim pointed to the coffee maker. "Coffee's ready."

At the kitchen table, leaning over her coffee cup, Pat said, "I'm going to meet with Melissa today."

"Connie's friend? Has Melissa heard from Connie?"

"I don't know. I suspect she's hoping Connie will reach out to her or me. We're meeting in Cambridge. You know the R&R in Inman Square?"

"Of course."

"That's where we're meeting. I'll come to your house afterwards."

Jim decided to walk to his house from Pat's. If he tired along the way, he could hop the Red Line or the Lechmere bus, but it was a nice day and he needed the exercise. He descended Beacon Hill to Charles Street, walked past its chi-chi shops to the arched Longfellow Bridge, and headed across the Charles. As he neared the middle of the bridge, the view widened dramatically, turning the river into a basin. On his right, the MIT dome. On his left, the Pru and Hancock towers. On the water, kayaks and sculls.

Jim stopped in the middle of the bridge to gaze. Where were Connie and Crankshaft? Somewhere in the Boston area? In New England? Or far away? He had no idea, of course, but an idea came into his head. Paris. Connie's brother, Timothy, lived there. A good place to hide.

He couldn't wait to tell Pat his idea.

He told her at dinner. She was skeptical to say the least.

"I don't see Connie leaving this country, with or without Crankshaft. I think she's adventurous within the framework of her upbringing but not beyond it."

Jim shrugged. "You know her better than I do."

"But I don't know her well enough to be sure. I could be wrong. Maybe she craved a total break from her past."

"How did your meeting with Melissa go?"

"She's very, very worried about Connie. Doesn't think Connie would drop completely out of sight on her own. She blames Crankshaft. We'll stay in touch."

Jim and Pat spent a restless night in Cambridge. A text from Timothy was waiting for Pat in the morning.

Booked on a flight to Boston tomorrow. Arriving 6 p.m. EST. Staying at the Carlton Hotel in Cambridge. Will call.

When Pat read the message out loud, Jim's response was, "That confirms that Connie's not in Paris."

"And that Timothy isn't faking his worry about her."

"Ask him what flight he'll be on. We can meet him at the airport."

*

The Air France flight was crowded, judging by the number of passengers deplaning. Jim stood with Pat, scrutinizing the passengers' faces.

A youngish but not youthful man blinked in the lights of the terminal. Pat looked at Jim with a question mark in her eyes. Jim nodded.

They approached him. "Timothy?"

He nodded. "You must be Pat Knowles. And you're Jim Randall."

"Yes, we are," Jim answered.

"The two of you are even more distinguished than I expected," Timothy said.

"Appearances deceive."

"Where can I get a cab?"

"I have my car. I can drop you off at your hotel," Jim said.

"Thank you," Timothy grunted.

"Did you check luggage?" Jim asked.

Timothy patted his backpack. "I travel light."

They walked to the garage. Logan airport was more difficult to navigate than usual because of construction, but eventually they were in Jim's car, driving through the tunnel to Storrow Drive, then across the river to Harvard Square. Timothy said little the whole trip.

"Here we are." Jim pulled up to the front door of the Carlton Hotel.

Pat said, "You'll want to rest up. Why don't we meet you for breakfast tomorrow?"

"Fine, but remember I'm still on Paris time. Why don't I call you?"

"Good," Pat said. As Timothy climbed out of the car, Pat said, "See you tomorrow."

Timothy grunted a goodbye.

"I don't like him," Pat said.

"Don't make snap judgements. Give him a chance."

"Based on his attitude, you'd think we were intruding."

"He's jet lagged, Pat."

"I'm taking that into account."

"How old would you say he is?"

"28, 30. Going on 65."

"You really don't like him, do you? I'm surprised. You usually withhold judgement."

"I want what's best for Connie, and I sense her brother may not be good for her. We don't know how she'll react when she learns he flew here to find her. But then again, we don't know where she is."

"You've really gone off the deep end," Jim said.

"Connie feels like the daughter I never had. A good kid. I want to help her."

"Her brother doesn't?"

"That remains to be seen."

Jim's townhouse came with a garage. A garage was a luxury in Cambridge. If he ever needed to supplement his pension, he could rent out his garage. He parked his car and they entered his townhouse.

They went to bed early. Reading in bed, Jim wondered what about Timothy grated so on Pat? He wanted to ask but her eyes were closed. He dozed and was about to fall into a deep sleep when the book Pat had been reading tumbled to the floor, waking them both.

"I must have fallen asleep," Pat said.

"We both did."

"I fell asleep trying to understand what about Timothy I distrust. I sense he harbors grudges."

"I don't sense that."

"You don't sense he's an angry man?"

"Well, his sister *is* missing."

"No, a fundamentally angry man. Not just about Connie. That's why I don't like him," Pat said.

"He seems benign to me. And I don't blame him for being worried."

"He'll worry about his sister until worrying about her gets in his way, that's what I think," Pat said.

They met Timothy for breakfast the next morning. As usual, the Carlton Hotel restaurant was crowded with academics trying without success to resolve anything. Pat and Jim approached Timothy's table. He looked fresh-faced and ready-to-go.

He smiled at them. "Mornin'. I'm still a little jet-lagged but not as bad as yesterday. Did you guys get any sleep?"

Jim answered for them. "We did, eventually, thank you."

Timothy showed them his phone. "I fell asleep last night without texting Connie I was here. I told her this morning and got this reply."

"So you've been in contact with her?"

"She hadn't replied to my texts until this morning. My flying here to look for her did the trick, I think. Take a look."

You're in Cambridge? I hate you. Why didn't you tell me you were coming? Stay where you are. I'll meet you there.

"She's coming to the hotel now. Wait here," Timothy said, getting to his feet. "If she's okay with it, I'll bring her to the restaurant."

He left, leaving Jim and Pat in shock.

"Wait? What just happened?" Jim asked.

"Timothy, who just arrived from Paris, is about to reunite with Connie, his sister, who had gone missing. Just the usual morning in Cambridge."

Two cups of coffee later, Timothy reappeared, this time with both Connie *and* Andy in tow.

Connie apologized as she sat down. "We didn't mean to cause so much trouble, guys, I just wanted to get away. To give me and Andy time to plan our future together. Timothy told me he flew from Paris to find me. I'm so, so sorry to cause so much trouble."

Pat gestured to the empty chairs. "Join us."

Andy looked chagrined and aggrieved, ready to fight or apologize. Without his Crankshaft getup, he had a Charlie Brown face, round cheeks and weightless hair.

He chose apology. "Sorry about all this. We needed time alone." His voice grated.

Pat signaled for coffee for the table. Andy continued, "Connie and I have been hiding in Somerville to have time to think. Connie deserves that."

She tried to be light-hearted, "We didn't know we'd be so missed."

Sternly, Pat banged her invisible gavel. "Now you know, both of you."

Jim played the conciliator, an unusual role for him. "Andy, I must say, you play a convincing villain in your videos."

Andy smiled. "It sells songs."

Connie patted his hand. "Don't be fooled, Andy's a softie at heart."

"That's not true," Andy stiffened.

She patted his hand again. "I'm exaggerating, babe. Relax."

Sheepishly, Andy tried to explain, "The role I play on stage is the person I'd like to be in real life if I weren't such a wimp." His fleeting smile slid behind his lips as quickly as it had appeared.

Jim had been content to sit back and observe, but the conversation had arrived at an inflection point. "How did you wind up in Paris?" he asked Timothy.

"The band I was playing with was offered a month's gig there. It turned into steady work, and I stayed."

That intrigued Andy. "What kind of music?"

"Quiet jazz. I play bass. We're good but unoriginal."

"I envy you. You have steady work in the city of light, I have to fight for every click in tired gray Boston."

With her natural air of authority, Pat took charge. "Connie, the authorities have to be notified that you're alive and well. Which of you will contact them?"

"Will Connie be in trouble?" Timothy asked.

"Not if she is forthright about where she's been and why she dropped out of touch, but be prepared for pushback, Connie. You've put a lot of people through a lot of worry for nothing. That won't sit well with some."

"Andy, will you come with me?" Connie asked.

"Of course, but when they see my videos, they may get the wrong impression."

Jim spoke for the first time, "Once Connie apologies I doubt if anyone is going to look at Andy's videos."

Pat counseled, "I wouldn't be so sure. Ted's thorough as hell."

"But Connie should apologize, whatever the fallout."

"I will," Connie said. "I'll explain what I did and why. Just tell me who to talk to."

"Whom," Pat corrected.

"Okay, whom."

"Ted Conover, the Assistant District Attorney who essentially runs the office. I'll tell him to expect to hear from you. And, Connie, you have to contact your father."

"I'm dreading that."

"I can see why, but he needs to know you're okay."

*

Jim and Pat were having dinner at Duck, Duck, Goose that evening when Pat's phone vibrated.

Pat stood when she saw who was calling. "It's Ted for me," she told Jim. "I'll take it outside."

Through the street window, Jim could watch Pat talking on the phone. She was not an animated talker – she shifted her weight from time to time but otherwise stood completely still. The call went on longer than Jim expected. Finally, Pat reentered the restaurant, bringing with her a burst of outside air, not to be confused with fresh air.

"Well?" Jim asked as Pat sat.

"Ted's on board. He was skeptical at first that Connie's disappearance was voluntary but I convinced him."

Jim nodded. "I'm not surprised. Skeptical but persuadable; that's Ted."

"I'll tell Connie tomorrow."

"Good. That ends it for us."

Pat demurred. "I doubt it."

5

A week later this headline appeared in the ***Boston Globe***:

Hiker falls to his death in White Mountains

The dead hiker was Timothy Hawkins, Connie's brother.

Jim was first to see the headline. "Take a look." He slid the paper across the kitchen table to Pat. A moment later, a sharp intake of breath.

"How awful," Pat exclaimed. "Connie told me that Timothy wanted to go mountain hiking, which he couldn't do in Paris, and that Andy offered to go with him." She slid the paper back to Jim. "I can't read the rest. Tell me what it says."

Jim read. When he finished, he looked across the table at Pat. "Andy was the one who reported the fall. The trail Timothy and Andy were on was known to be treacherous.."

"Has the body been recovered?"

"Yes. No evidence of foul play. It looks like an accident. You should reach out to Connie."

"And you to Andy/Crankshaft."

Connie was too distraught to talk. Crankshaft was eager to talk.

He met Jim out of makeup at The Long Gone.

The morning crowd had thinned. As Andy, Crankshaft looked abject, lost.

"Sorry I'm late."

Jim checked his watch. "You're not late."

"I thought I was."

"If you want coffee, you have to order it at that counter." Jim pointed.

"I don't drink coffee. No stimulants, no downers." Andy checked his surroundings. "Do you think anybody recognizes me?"

Jim said, "How could they? Out of makeup, you don't look at all like the guy in the videos."

"You'd be surprised how obsessive fans can be. I know of more than one girl who collects photos of me out of makeup. I don't understand it, to be honest."

"Your public persona grabs attention."

"I get that. Attention's what I want, but obsession?"

"I'm sure it's painful to talk about, but tell me what happened on the mountain."

Crankshaft shook his head. Jim couldn't read the gesture: was he trying to grasp the horror of what happened or was he too upset to talk? "Timothy was walking ahead of me. If I'd been paying attention, maybe I could've stopped him from going over. Or at least tried, I blame myself for his death." He didn't sound very convincing. His words were the correct ones under the circumstances, but his affect, his demeanor, was flat. Maybe that was just Andy's way of dealing with tragedy that wasn't staged.

"I don't think you should blame yourself. I doubt you could have stopped him."

Andy grew agitated. "You don't know that! I could've warned him to step back from the edge! I could've grabbed him before he went over!"

"It was ruled an accident by the medical examiner."

"Who wasn't there!"

"Is there a possibility Timothy wanted to die?"

"Are you suggesting suicide? How dare you? How fuckin' dare you? Connie says he loved his life. No, his death is my fault, I'm to blame, my fault, I'm to blame."

There was something robotic about the response that struck Jim as staged in spite of Andy being out of makeup. "Connie isn't angry at you. Doesn't that tell you something?"

"I can't believe Connie'll have anything to do with me after this. She's a genuinely good person and I'm not."

A college-age woman approached Crankshaft and sheepishly asked, "Excuse me. Are you who I think you are?"

Crankshaft looked up. "Depends if you think I'm Jake Gyllenhaal. If not, then no."

The young woman looked embarrassed. "You're not Crankshaft? I've downloaded all your videos. I love them."

"Thank you."

"I knew it! You are Crankshaft! I can't believe I'm meeting you. Will your friend take a picture of us together?"

Jim answered, "I'm sorry. I don't know how."

"I'll snap a selfie. May I?" And she leaned down so her head was next to Andy's and took a selfie before he could say yay or nay. "Thank you, thank you!" she said as she waved goodbye.

Jim waited until the dust settled. "Do you get that a lot?" he asked Crankshaft.

"I'm rarely recognized out of costume."

"She certainly recognized you."

"Some fans...I don't understand that level of devotion, I crave it but don't understand it."

*

At Pat's apartment that night: "I spoke to Connie today. She's too distraught to be coherent."

"You've done what you can, Pat."

"I know. But it makes me sad."

They ate a quick dinner in Pat's kitchen watching the PBS Newshour. Jim kept a supply of wine at Pat's apartment, mostly red. French table wines were more than adequate at $15-20 a bottle, no need to spend big money. He chose a Corbières.

He raised his glass. "Here's to Connie Hawkins. May she find ways to cope with her loss."

He and Pat drank and put down their glasses. Pat's phone buzzed.

She checked the text and jumped up from the table. "It's Connie. She's coming here. She sounds awful."

"Where is she?"

"On her way. I worry she'll get lost. She's only been to my apartment once."

Pat hurried to the front door. The street was dark and quiet. "Connie!" Pat called outside. "Here!"

Connie appeared in the doorway a moment later, out-of-breath. "He killed Timothy, didn't he?"

"Who?" Pat asked.

"Andy! My Andy! Crankshaft! Who do you think?"

Pat took Connie by the arm. "Come inside."

Connie collapsed in Pat's living room. "Andy clammed up when I couldn't stop asking questions. If he has nothing to hide, he'd wouldn't get defensive, would he? Oh, God, oh, God."

Pat sat down beside Connie. "Talk to me, Connie. Let it out."

A torrent of words followed. "Andy fell asleep as soon as he got home from the mountains. The next thing I know he was sitting up sobbing. It was horrible to see. My fault, my fault! he kept repeating. I had never seen Andy sob before."

"What happened next?" Pat asked.

"Andy put on his shoes and ran out of my apartment. I didn't know what to do, so I came here. Tell me what to do."

"Do you have any idea where Andy would go?"

"None, don't you see? That's the problem!" Connie got hysterical again.

Pat soothed her. "Okay, let's slow down, Connie."

"I called Andy's bandmates but they have no idea where he is!" Connie started to stand. Pat tried to stop her. "Let me go! I have to be home in case Andy comes looking for me."

Connie hurried out the door. Her absence was so sudden and her presence so brief, it was as if she had never been there.

Jim and Pat counted their senses to be sure they still had six. Jim: "I have an impression that Connie was just here. Was I hallucinating?"

"No, but I think she was."

"A memorable evening," Jim said.

"For sure. I never saw this side of Connie while I was mentoring her. She defined nose-to-the-grindstone, always studying. Borderline hysterical? Never."

"That's a little harsh. Neither of us knows what we'd do in her situation."

"True, but allow me to vent."

He touched her Pat's elbow. "Of course. Vent all you want."

"No, I'm done. Back to being the staid yet kind-hearted Judge Knowles, former justice of the Superior Court, ardent lover of curmudgeonly Judge Randall. Better?"

"Now you're talking."

*

Two things happened almost simultaneously a week later: Andy reappeared and Connie apologized to her father for disappearing.

Andy explained why he had fled: "I'm sorry, Connie. Things had been moving too fast, I needed time to think. He promised his head was now on straight.

Connie's dad was apoplectic about her disappearance and relieved to hear from her in equal measure; she and he had not fully cleared the air by the time of Timothy's funeral.

Timothy was buried at Mt. Auburn Cemetery. Before the burial, a memorial service was held in the cemetery's small chapel.

Connie spoke for her father, who was too distraught to speak. "My brother had so much heart, so much kindness. I can't believe he's gone. Rest in peace, dear brother."

After the service, Jim and Pat spoke outside the chapel.

"That was painful," Jim said.

"Very," Pat echoed.

They reached Jim's car. "Maybe now life can return to normal," Jim offered once seated.

Pat shook her head. "I'd like to think so, but I doubt it."

6

Two weeks later, in Pat's apartment – "Connie called me again. That makes two times since she reappeared. Each time she says she wants to talk, then when she's about to unburden herself, she backs off, acts as if nothing has changed. She feels guilty about something, but I'm losing patience. I was her mentor, not her mother. Should I tell her to stop calling me?"

"Don't you dare. She needs you as a confidant and I need your eyes and ears."

"Lovely. You need my eyes and ears. That's all?"

"You know what I mean."

"I do and I will, keep encouraging her, that is."

Jim needed a walk on Beauty Shop Row to ground him, so after his morning coffee at The Long Gone, he continued down Cambridge Street towards the Lechmere T station. Jim had dubbed that stretch of street Beauty Shop Row because never in his wildest imagination (if he had ever thought about it, which he hadn't) could he have imagined that so many shops could be devoted to hair, skin, and eyebrows on the street between Harvard and MIT, or anywhere for that matter. And men weren't neglected. Barber shops were on that stretch of Cambridge Street too. None were called barber shops, per se; they were emporiums or better yet, palaces. Jim had unruly hair that he didn't notice until Pat dubbed him Einstein, not for his brains but his hair. He then would get it cut at a barber shop. No adjectives, no additives. Scissors and razors. A barber shop.

He passed Rosie's House of Beauty, Sandra's Hair and Nails, and as he passed Skin R Us, a path ahead came to mind: Pat would continue being Connie's confident, while Jim would get to know Crankshaft and his world. Jim turned and caught a #69 bus home to tell Pat.

"It will be a joint effort, you and me. What do you think?" he asked Pat at his townhouse.

"We always collaborate on cases."

"But not officially. This case will be billed as Pat and Jim's Incredible Adventure."

"As long as you leave the 'ah ha' moment for me."

"A little competitive, are we?"

"A little insecure, art thou?" Pat answered.

They were about to get into bed.

"Why am I not with a compliant woman?" Jim said.

That made Pat burst out laughing.

*

Jim was out of touch with the subdivisions of heavy metal (joke: he had never been in touch with any subdivision of heavy metal...nor punk, hip hop, or rap for that matter). With Ernie's help he identified the local bars that featured music of Crankshaft's genre. One was in Central Square (The Shattered Glass). He wanted to immerse himself in Crankshaft's world, which was his standard modus vivendi (get to know the world of your suspect and a solution will follow). He could walk to Central Square but he felt lazy so he took the T.

"Want to come?" he asked Pat before he left.

"No. I'll give a lot for the cause, but not my eardrums."

The Shattered Glass in Jim's day would've been dubbed 'smoky,' but smoking having been banned in clubs long ago, it now could be called 'stuffy,' 'rancid' and/or 'claustrophobic.' He was glad Pat had decided not to come because she had a touch of claustrophobia.

A recorded beat was pounding when Jim walked in. He was at least four decades older than anyone else in the club which made him self-conscious, until he realized no one seemed to mind or even notice. When the recorded music was replaced by a live band, the pile driver beat pierced his body like a spear. His eardrums stood no chance. Why had he come? What had he been thinking?

On the band's break, a young woman standing shoulder-to-shoulder with him asked, "Do you like this kind of music?" She was with a shy young man who refused to look at Jim.

Jim wasn't sure how to answer. "Honestly, I don't know it; I'm here to learn."

She nodded, not buying his explanation. "Un huh," she said.

For some reason, Jim wanted her to understand. "No, really. I recently heard of a singer named Crankshaft – do you know him? Have you heard of him?"

"Crankshaft? Of course. I see him here from time to time."

"I'd like to find him."

"You want to find Crankshaft?" The young woman nudged her companion. "Wilson, he wants to find Crankshaft."

Jim couldn't hear the boyfriend's response but the young woman relayed it as, had Jim tried The Night Shift?

"The Night Shift?"

"A bar in North Cambridge. Crankshaft hangs out there when he's not playing elsewhere."

"That's good to know."

The young woman offered her hand. "My name's Lucy."

"I'm Jim. Jim Randall." To cover his embarrassment he added, "I used to be a judge."

"Pleased to meet you." She nudged her boyfriend. "He used to be a judge."

Jim wasn't used to meeting young women under these circumstances (or any circumstances, for that matter) and he offered this non-sequitur: "The music I grew up with was quite a bit different. Miles, Coltrane, Dylan."

Lucy nodded.

"Have you heard of them?" Jim asked.

"Bob Dylan. I've heard of him."

"Miles Davis and John Coltrane were my jazz heroes." (Shut up, Jim, he scolded himself.)

She didn't want to be rude, nor did she want to pretend she knew who Jim was talking about. Lucy's boyfriend was restless. Jim wanted to save him the trouble of prying Lucy away, and Jim wanted to save his eardrums.

Jim looked for a path through the crowd. "Nice talking to you."

"You're leaving? Remember, The Night Shift."

*

Mass Ave near the Arlington line still looked city-like but the suburbs encroached. The Night Shift looked derelict. A small light hung above the door, the name Night Shift barely visible.

Jim opened the door with trepidation and was greeted by a noise that sounded like a cross between a gang fight and a train wreck.

A young man at the door said, "Need help?"

"Is Crankshaft playing here tonight?"

"You want to see Crankshaft's band?"

"I want to talk to him."

"He's not here yet."

"I'll stick around as long as my eardrums can take it."

The young man shrugged. "Suit yourself."

Jim went to the bar and ordered red wine.

"We got handcrafted beer. We got local IPA. We got gin."

"No wine?"

"White only. No red."

"I'll take an IPA."

The bartender spun away and returned carrying a mug of draft ale. "Long Trail. Brewed in Vermont. Tell me if you like it."

Jim took a sip. "Not bad."

There was a pause in the recorded music. During the pause a tech came on stage to test the mics. The stage was a small platform raised an inch or two off the floor. One by one, the musicians appeared, tested their instruments, and disappeared again.

The unsuspecting would have no idea what was about to hit them. When the musicians returned a few moments later and started to pound, heads bobbed and bowels shook. Miles Davis this wasn't. Anger was the driving force, not musicality. What did today's kids have to be so angry about? Then again, his generation had been angry too; for what reason he couldn't remember, the pile driver beat rendering memory moot.

Jim, drinking his ale, tried to focus on why he was here. Partly curiosity about Crankshaft, partly a desire to help Pat with Connie, partly because he hated playing second fiddle, which was probably not the metaphor to use in a heavy metal bar.

He felt a tap on his shoulder. "Are you the man who's looking for Crankshaft?"

Jim turned his head to see who it was. "Someone wants to see you backstage," a self-conscious young man said.

"Who?" Jim said.

"Come with me, please."

The young man led Jim through a side door and down a short hall to a room cluttered with stage equipment. Andy was sitting at a makeshift mirror applying his Crankshaft makeup. He applied the finishing touch, then turned to Jim.

"I'm surprised to see you here," he said.

"Not as surprised as I am to be here," Jim replied.

Andy/Crankshaft held up his finger to tell Jim to wait, then pulled out his phone and placed a call. "Hey," he said, when someone answered. "Guess who's here?" He handed the phone to Jim.

A woman's voice. "I didn't think you were serious."

"Who is this? Connie?"

"Yes, it's me. We thought you were playing with us."

"I don't play with death."

"I'm sorry, Judge Randall. Do you forgive me?"

"There's nothing to forgive. You're under great stress."

Crankshaft interrupted. "I'm about to go onstage. Can I speak to Connie again?"

"Andy wants to speak to you before he goes on," Jim said over the phone. To Andy, he said, "I'll be in the audience."

Jim went out front and got ready for the onslaught, but nothing could prepare him for the pile driver beat when it began. All traces of Andy were erased by Crankshaft in full-demon mode, glaring, screaming, and prancing across stage. Crankshaft had become real; Andy was now make-believe.

Jim stayed as long as his eardrums allowed, then drove home shakily.

7

Waking up next to Pat in the morning – in his bedroom on a quiet mid-Cambridge street – Jim needed a moment to shake the incessant beat from his head.

"The anger, the anger," he marveled when Pat saw him shaking his head.

Pat struggled upright. "What are you talking about?"

"Crankshaft. I assume much of his act is for effect, but good god!"

"Are you now his groupie?"

Jim didn't answer. He had a thought: "Timothy's death was ruled an accident, I can drop this case, can't I?"

"You can."

"No more Crankshaft, right?"

"That's right."

"I don't have to subject myself to his 'music.'"

"Correct."

"So why can't I get Crankshaft out of my head?"

"You have become a groupie."

"No, seriously, Pat. Why don't I ditch this case?"

"Besides being a touch obsessive-compulsive, not to mention congenitally stubborn? Besides that?"

"I'm serious, Pat. The way I've reacted to this case troubles me in so many ways. I have totally lost my objectivity."

"But no harm done. The medical examiner has ruled it was an accident. You're off the hook."

Jim got out of bed and put on his usual khakis. "I'm going downstairs. I'll put the coffee on."

"I'll be down in a minute."

He was on his second cup of coffee when Pat appeared in the kitchen.

"Took you long enough," he commented.

"Well, it's quicker to get dressed when one always wears the same thing."

"I don't like thinking about clothes."

She poured herself a cup of coffee. "Could've fooled me, the snappy way you dress."

"My signature look. Khakis and work shirts. Distinctive."

Pat kissed Jim on the top of his head and sat down at the breakfast table. "You're cute."

"That's what the criminals I sent to jail used to say as they were led from the courtroom: 'Judge Randall, you're cute. No hard feelings.'"

"That's what they said?"

"Word for word."

Pat was on her second cup of coffee when she continued. As was her wont, her words were carefully considered. "I think I've gained Connie's trust. If she has anything else to reveal, I think I'll be the one she'll reveal it to."

"Keep at it."

"And you, my dear, it's Crankshaft for you."

Jim grimaced. "I realize. My eardrums cringe."

"Too bad you didn't meet him while you were still a judge. You'd look good in makeup and mask. Picture it: you on the bench as Crankshaft."

Jim laughed. "Defendants would have been terrified."

"They would have plead guilty and begged for mercy." Pat stood to get more coffee. "Didn't you wish you could scream at defendants some of the time? I know I did."

"Yes, and lawyers. Especially lawyers."

"Presiding as Crankshaft would have given you license to scream." Pat filled her cup. "More coffee?" she asked Jim. When he didn't answer, Pat nudged him. "Jim?"

"What?"

"More coffee?"

"No, thanks. Here's my thinking: I'm not entirely convinced by the coroner's verdict and I don't think you are either. I doubt we will be until we unravel the personalities of the major players. We're making progress but the jigsaw puzzle isn't complete. Crankshaft is playing again tonight at the Night Shift and I shall be there."

While sitting on a bar stool that night waiting for Crankshaft to come on, Jim made a mental comparison of Ipsa Loquitur and the Night Shift. After failing (there was no similarity between legal laughter and pile driver beats), he gave up and concentrated on the stage, waiting for Crankshaft.

He caught the bartender's attention. "What time does Crankshaft usually go on?"

"The word 'usually' doesn't exist in Crankshaft's vocabulary. He comes and goes as he pleases. There's no back entrance so you'll see him when he comes in."

The bartender went about his business but circled back a moment later. "Do you know him?" he asked Jim incredulously. "You don't look like the kind of man who would know Crankshaft."

"I've met him. I don't know him well."

"No one knows Crankshaft well, he stays in character on- and off-stage." The bartender shrugged. "But hey, we're all playing parts, aren't we? Some are just more extreme than others."

A woman at the far end of the bar signaled for another beer. The bartender nodded and walked the length of the bar.

Beckett's two tramps waited for Godot, how many senior citizens ever sat on a bar stool waiting for Crankshaft?

Jim texted Pat to tell her he was at the Night Shift waiting for Crankshaft. Jim drummed his thumbs on the bar. The bartender approached.

"Crankshaft wants to see you."

"Where do I go?"

"Through that door."

Jim left his ale on the bar and went in back looking for Crankshaft. He found him in the makeshift dressing room applying his satanic makeup.

"You wanted to see me?" Jim began.

"Every time you see me I'm putting on my stage makeup. Why are you here? What do you want from me?"

"I'm learning a new version of reality by watching you on stage."

Andy considered that for a second, then shook his head. "Bullshit." He turned again to the mirror. "This is the finishing touch." Andy smeared black paint under his eyes and on his lips. "Scared yet?" He bared his teeth which looked remarkably white against the black makeup.

"No. Are you scared?"

Crankshaft laughed. He stood and stretched. "Done. Gird your eardrums." As he headed out front, he asked, "You're actually going to stick around for another night of screaming?"

"Wouldn't miss it for the world."

"I can't eat before I go on or I throw up. After I get off we can go to the twenty-four hour diner around the corner, if you're still here."

The music was explosive, i.e., ear shattering. Note to self: remember to bring earplugs next time. Listening to the pounding and shrieking, Jim's mind wandered. Jim told himself that if his mind could wander in the presence of such noise, he was getting used to it. Horrible thought: was he beginning to like heavy metal?

After the set, it took Andy almost as long to remove his Crankshaft makeup as it had to put it on. When Andy Taylor emerged from the back, fresh-faced but exhausted, very few people recognized him. Which didn't seem to faze him.

"Whew!" Andy said. "Especially savage crowd tonight." He and Jim left the bar. "The diner I told you about is a block away. Okay?"

Jim was winded from absorbing the pile driver beat. When he mentioned that to Andy, Andy said, "How do you think I feel?"

The diner had the melancholy feel of a Hopper painting. Andy slid into a booth. "Food, food," he muttered.

"You were ferocious tonight," Jim said.

"I'm good at it." He glanced at a menu. "Judge, I like you and I think you like me, but I want you to leave me the fuck alone. I didn't kill Timothy and I'm tired of being stalked. No offense."

"I detect a guilty conscience."

"Eggs over easy, bacon and coffee, black," Andy told the waitress.

"Toast with that?"

"English muffin."

"And you, sir?" the waitress asked Jim.

"Just coffee."

"Cream and sugar?"

"No, black."

Jim and Andy fell silent when the waitress had gone. Andy was exhausted from his performance, Jim because he was old.

The coffee came.

Jim roused himself. "I'll stop stalking you – as you put it – when you tell me what really happened on that trail. The truth. I'm listening."

"I've told you the truth. We were on a very narrow trail high in the White Mountains. Timothy got too close to the edge. I tried to warn him – 'you're too close!' but I was too late. My shame, my fault. He slipped, I lunged...." Andy shook his head in shame and sorrow. His eyes glistened. "I'll never forget seeing him go over the edge." Andy looked up at Jim. "Do you believe me?"

"One thing a judge learns to do is to withhold judgement until all the facts are in."

"But I was the only eyewitness and I'm telling you what I saw, so those are the facts! Why don't you believe me?"

"Because you're lying."

The diner seemed to go silent, as if it had emptied of people. Was Jim having a seizure? A stroke? Then the noise resumed – louder than the traffic hum, quieter than Crankshaft's band in the Night Shift.

"You are persistent, I'll give you that, but you have been warned. Leave me alone."

"Who is threatening me? Crankshaft or Andy?"

The waitress brought Andy's food.

"Eggs over easy, English muffin. More coffee?" she asked the two of them.

"Please," Andy said. Jim shook his head no.

Andy ate faster than Jim had seen anybody eat. While he ate, a torrent of words spilled from his mouth. "Why would I kill him? Why? No one has been able to give me a plausible reason. Why *would* I kill him? Tell me?"

"That's not how it works, Andy. You tell me. You had your reasons. Assuming you pushed Timothy, why did you? Enlighten me."

Andy shrugged convincingly. "That's just it, there's no reason. Even if I hated him, which I didn't. I hardly knew him. Timothy was living in Paris while I was getting to know Connie. Why would I kill a guy I barely knew?"

"You're a hothead, Andy. That's why you chose Crankshaft as your alter ego. Crankshaft gives you permission to be yourself."

Andy shook his head. "And you were once a judge? Is that the best you can do?"

"As long as Timothy stayed in Paris, he was no threat, but when he arrived in the states, you feared he would see through you and warn Connie of your real nature."

Did Andy just flinch or was that Jim's imagination? No rush, let it play out. Jim slipped a five-dollar bill from his wallet and placed it on the table. He stood. "This is for my coffee. Have a good night, Andy." Put the noose around a suspect's neck, then take a break. Let him sweat.

"You're leaving?" Andy seemed panicky.

"I am. I'm going home to my comfortable bed next to the woman I love, where I predict I will sleep like a baby, untroubled by a guilty conscience."

Jim left the diner. At first he couldn't remember where he had parked his car, but as he started walking, he remembered.

As he walked, he knew in his ex-judge's bones that *Andy Taylor* was the disguise, not Crankshaft. Why did Jim feel that so strongly tonight? He sensed fear in Andy, fear of being exposed for who he really was. Andy's shyness had seemed artificial from the moment they met. Andy Taylor had constructed his personality so well, melding bits of shyness with glimpses of openness, that he seemed more cyborg than human. Jim could understand Andy's fear at Timothy's return from Paris. Who better to warn Connie that Andy was not the good guy he seemed than Timothy, her brother?

Jim entered his house as quietly as he could so as not to wake Pat. Pat opened her eyes when Jim crawled into bed beside her.

"I didn't mean to wake you."

"What time is it?"

Jim checked his clock. "Almost two."

"You're just getting home?"

"Yes."

"How did you manage to stay awake this long?"

"The noise insisted."

"Poor Jim. Did you learn anything?"

"Buy earplugs."

"Is that all?"

"And Andy's one of the most sincere-sounding liars I've known since my judging days, but he is a liar nonetheless. I have no proof, only my instinct but I'm sure."

"Are you saying you think he's guilty of murder?"

"I think the medical examiner may have been premature in calling Timothy's death an accident. Have you learned anything new from Connie?"

"No. Nothing. She's convinced it was an accident because she wants to be convinced. She refuses to accept the possibility that her boyfriend killed her brother."

"Who can blame her?"

"What are you thinking?" Pat asked after several minutes of silence.

"That I'd love to see the trail where Timothy fell, but I'm too damn old."

"Agreed. I'm in better shape than you, but it's supposedly a dangerous trail."

"Who says you're in better shape than me?"

"Anyone with eyes. You need rest. Go to sleep."

*

Jim stopped by Ted's office the next day.

"Thanks for seeing me on such short notice," Jim said.

"Always a pleasure."

"Pat and I are still examining the evidence in Timothy Hawkins's death, which as you know the New Hampshire medical examiner declared accidental."

"And because you are the suspicious type, you don't believe him."

"Because I was a judge for twenty-one years."

"I.e, the suspicious type."

"Have you talked to your NH counterpart about the trail Timothy and Andy were on before Timothy fell?"

"Yes."

"And?"

"He says the trail is narrow but not deadly. Trail maps clearly label the trail as for 'Experienced Hikers,' which both Timothy and Andy were."

"So it's unlikely an experienced hiker would accidentally fall off the trail?"

"Highly unlikely."

"Did the New Hampshire DA consider the possibility that Timothy Hawkins was pushed?"

"Of course, that was one of the first things he considered, but there's no such evidence. None. Andy Taylor claims to have been several feet behind Timothy; he was the only eyewitness and there is no forensic evidence to contradict his story."

"No signs of a struggle?"

"None, nor any evidence that rain had eroded the trail to such an extent that the edge would collapse when a hiker walked too close. The trail was in good shape."

Jim pointed behind Ted. "When are you going to hang a new painting on your goddamn wall?"

Ted swiveled in his chair to look. In the faded and cracked oil painting a sailboat leaned into the wind on a choppy sea. "Why should I?"

"It dates you. Makes you seem old and tired."

"'Projection,' Jim."

Jim's walk home took him past the hair salons and skin emporiums of Beauty Shop Row but for a change he barely noticed. His mind was on a high mountain trail. He had no reason to doubt the official explanation for Timothy's death except for two things: instinct and hope, instinct that Andy was a bad guy and hope that Connie was not in danger from him. Why did he care? He hated to see anybody get away with murder, that's why. And he liked Connie. True, Pat had been the one who mentored her, but Jim liked her.

Pat was absorbed in her laptop at the kitchen table when he got home.

"Hi, what are you doing?"

She answered without looking up. "Writing a reference for a former colleague. How did it go?"

"Good to see Ted."

She looked up from her laptop. "Not well, huh?"

"Accident remains the official verdict. Is there any coffee left?"

"I think so."

He checked. There was. He poured himself a cup, took a sip and let out a sigh. "It's a long walk from Ted's office and I'm not getting any younger. Are you aware that I'm aging? Be careful of your answer."

"Jim, you are always young in my eyes."

"Good answer."

"Of course, my eyes are worsening by the day."

He chuckled.

Pat continued. "Jim, I know you have doubts about Timothy's death. I have doubts of my own, but we must not be overly stubborn. Connie needs to heal and for that, she needs closure."

"You're probably right. The medical examiner says it was an accident, Andy says it was an accident...."

"But you still have doubts. You know I admire your instincts, but think of Connie."

"Look, the odds are Andy's telling the truth about Timothy – when he talks about his plunge he seems genuinely broken up – but any guy who can so convincingly play a villain can fake being broken up. Anyway, all I've got to lose are my eardrums. Which reminds me: buy earplugs."

"You plan to hear Crankshaft again?"

"I do. Who knows? If I start chanting his lyrics, call for help."

8

There had been a time not so long ago when Jim wouldn't think twice about donning hiking boots and setting out on the suspect trail. Not anymore; his legs sent unmistakable signals of 'don't even think of it.' He hated – truly hated – not being able to walk wherever he wanted, but he could go to his Vermont house and look across the river at New Hampshire, couldn't he? Hey, almost the same thing as climbing a mountain in New Hampshire, right?

"Want to come?"

"Sure," Pat said. Jim could never predict what she'd say. Even after knowing her as a colleague for years and co-habiting with her long enough for it to become the norm, he still couldn't predict when she'd want to come to Vermont with him and when she wouldn't.

"I'm going to be preoccupied," Jim warned her.

"When are you not?"

"Especially preoccupied, I mean."

"I know you, Jim. You don't have to spell everything out."

They drove up on a Tuesday to avoid the weekend traffic. Not that the traffic on the rural part of Route 2 was ever bumper-to-bumper, but there could be enough to annoy Jim (which didn't take much). Today the traffic was its usual busy but flowing self.

"Any special reason for the timing of this visit?" Pat looked dignified no matter where she was, even sitting in his passenger seat. Not stuffy, never stuffy: Pat could go from salt-of-the-earth to dignified without passing stuffy. "I'm looking for luck," he said as he navigated the wide curve around Fitchburg.

"Any particular reason you say that now?" Pat asked.

"Damn drivers need to slow down around this damn curve."

"That's why you're looking for luck?"

They emerged from the curve.

"I feel lucky you'll have anything to do with me. I'm stubborn, old, and irritable."

"Good."

"You are glad I'm stubborn, old, and irritable?"

"No, I'm glad to hear you say that about yourself. Self-awareness is not usually your thing."

"Vermont beings out the soul-searcher in me."

"We're still in Massachusetts."

"You would have made a superb fact checker."

"I feel the same about you."

"I would've made a good fact checker?"

"No, I feel lucky to be with you. I'm not always sure why, but I am."

They reached the shortcut at Irving. Jim drove slowly out of respect for the residents who lived on the winding, undulating back road, one of his favorite back roads anywhere.

"Where are you in your thinking about Timothy's death?" Pat asked as they approached Northfield.

"I feel awful for Connie and I'm intrigued and flummoxed by Crankshaft."

Pat nodded. "Connie can't talk about Timothy's death without sobbing. If you see a puddle, don't step in it. It could be Connie."

As always, when Jim opened the front door, his Vermont house smelled of stale air and mouse droppings. And as always, the first thing he did inside the house was go to the long windows in the living room and gaze at the Connecticut River in its shallow valley. Today the river was shrouded in low clouds. New Hampshire – relatively flat this far south of the White Mountains – was the landscape Jim saw across the river.

He turned away from the window. "Nope."

"Nope what?"

"No solution there."

She came to stand beside him.

"Did you expect one?"

"I need to explain whimsey to you, Pat. Over dinner perhaps."

They ate at the nearby inn. The inn had good food and atmosphere, but he most liked the location – surrounded by trees but not in the dark. The maître d' welcomed them back and led them to a window table.

"You don't let others sit at this table when we're not here, do you?" Jim asked.

"Only ex-judges, with a preference for ex-judges in pairs." The maître d' deposited menus at their places and bid them a good meal.

They didn't discuss the case until they toasted each other.

"Not bad." Jim lowered his wine glass.

"What is it?"

"Côte du Luberon. You don't like it?"

"It's fine." She put it down.

He started to explain the wine's origin, but she cut him off.

"Connie is beginning to think as you do that Crankshaft is Andy's true personality, that the shy Andy she has loved is the disguise. The thought terrifies her. She wonders if she has been in danger this whole time."

"I hope not. I hope to be able to conclude my investigation soon."

For the rest of the evening they avoided talking about the case. When they got home they were tired, but before going to bed Jim stood at the long window, gazing at the sleeping Connecticut River. He found it amusing that the Green Mountain State and the Live Free Or Die State needed Connecticut to separate them.

The next morning, the first thing Pat said when she and Jim were awake was, "I woke up during the night convinced that Connie knows more than we realize. I've kept that thought at arm's length because I don't want to believe it."

"Something about Timothy's death?"

"Something she knows about Andy that we don't. Not that she's said anything, but that's how I read her. I could be totally wrong. Jim, how do you keep your feelings out of the cases you investigate?"

"Badly, but to the extent I do, I do it in the same way we removed our personal feelings from the cases we heard as judges. Experience and will power. No magic trick."

Pat had a distinctive shake of her head when she was annoyed; now she was annoyed with herself. "I've gotten too close to Connie."

"Don't beat yourself up. To sleuth is to fail. All we can do is keep trying. As Beckett said, 'fail again, fail better.'" Jim jumped out of bed. "I'm hungry."

They ate breakfast at the table by the long window. "How long do you plan to stay up here this time?" Pat asked.

"I don't have a plan. Why? Restless already? We've only been up here one night."

"Usually I'm on the sidelines. Not so in this case because I know Connie better than you and for her sake, I want to wrap this up. So how long do you think we'll stay up here?"

They drove back to Cambridge the next day, arriving at Jim's townhouse at noon. Jim was exhausted.

"Why?" Pat asked. "I drove half the way."

"But my half was more exhausting."

"You poor thing."

"In fact, I'm going upstairs to lie down," Jim said.

Jim fell asleep. He usually only dozed when he napped, but this time he fell fast asleep. Eventually Pat came upstairs to check on him. He awoke when he sensed her presence. "What's wrong?" he said.

"I just wanted to see if you were alive."

"I am." He pushed himself up on his elbows. "Happy?"

"Delighted. I'm meeting Connie in Harvard Square at thirty minutes. I'll be back in time for dinner."

While Pat was away, Jim called Ted.

"Pat and I just got back from Vermont. Anything new on the Timothy Hawkins case?"

"Welcome back. I didn't know you had been away. Nothing new here. We consider the Timothy Hawkins's case closed, but you've learned something new, haven't you?"

"Possibly. I think we've gone about this case the wrong way. Start with the improbable, then work our way back to the likely."

"Even more inscrutable than usual, Jim."

"Crankshaft is the real character, Andy Taylor is the avatar. Could Andy kill? Unlikely. Could Crankshaft? Without a doubt."

"That's all you've got?"

"For now. Ipsa Loquitur today after work?"

How was it possible that the noise in the Ipsa Loquitur never varied? Jim had long since decided that bar air came from a single supplier – StaleAir.com? Was it the same for bar noise? If so, was the noise streamed in or was it shipped in kegs? He had assumed that the kegs wheeled into bars contained beer but maybe some of them contained noise. Furthermore, if bar air and bar noise came from single sources, were the sources in danger of depletion, leaving bars with – perish the thought – fresh air and silence? Those questions could be his next project after crime-solving lost its charm.

Ted looked tired. "I'm getting too old for this," he said, his voice barely audible over the din.

"For drinking?"

Ted had been leaning against the bar. He pushed himself upright. "I shouldn't complain about age, but I will. I don't like aging. There, my secret is out."

"You've got nothing to complain about. You're a kid, I'm the codger."

Ted laughed. "Codger, absolutely. Doddering, actually."

"I dodder for no man." Jim leaned close to the barkeep. "A glass of your French red, please."

"Jim, you and Pat are so in sync that where one of you ends and the other begins is sometimes hard to see. How do you two manage when one of you has an ego like yours?"

"Who says I have an ego?"

"The entire legal profession of Eastern Massachusetts. Seriously, how do you two manage?"

"We respect each other so much that we are able to defer to the other when necessary. I'm usually right, though, as you know."

"Obviously. Who can disagree?"

The barkeep brought Jim his wine.

"Cheers." Jim lifted his glass. "I think the New Hampshire medical examiner may have gotten this one wrong. What strengthens that hunch is what Pat is learning from Connie Hawkins. Connie is growing scared of her boyfriend, Andy Taylor, who was with Timothy Hawkins when he fell to his death. Andy is not the nice guy he seems."

"Interesting theory in search of a shred of proof."

"I've beaten proof to the finish line in one or two previous cases, haven't I?"

"You have but that doesn't prove you're right in this case."

Jim shook his head. "Remember all the times I gaveled you to silence when you appeared in my court? Ah, those were the days. I'd give anything for a gavel. Where is my gavel? My kingdom for a gavel."

Jim didn't stay at the Ipsa Loquitur much longer; even so, he got to Pat's apartment past dinnertime.

"Did you eat?" she asked when he arrived.

"I forgot."

"Are you hungry?"

"Got anything in the refrigerator I could nibble on?"

"I've never heard you say 'nibble' before. You should say it more often. It suits you."

"Nibble, nibble, nibble," Jim chanted on the way to the kitchen.

"Perfect. Set that to a beat and you've got yourself a hit."

"What will my stage name be?"

"DJ Rough Justice."

Jim went to the kitchen and returned with a plate of bread, cheese, and carrot sticks.

"That's not going to be enough for you," Pat said.

"Yes, it will."

Jim lay awake that night listening to the distant hum of traffic, imagining for the umpteenth time what could be Andy's motive for pushing Timothy off the mountain – if he had, that is? Did Timothy know something about Andy that could land Andy in jail? Did Andy resent the close ties between Timothy and his sister? Was Andy afraid Timothy was going to turn Connie against him? Murders had been committed for more far-fetched reasons than that.

He fell asleep without an answer and was still mulling motive when he woke up in the morning, pleased to have only gotten up once during the night.

Jim slid out of bed as silently as he could so as not to awaken Pat and went downstairs to make coffee. He had to adjust his morning routine to her kitchen whenever he slept over, and sometimes got it wrong. Routine was the last thing that would die when he expired, not heartbeat, not breath. Routine. He opened the wrong cabinet looking for a coffee cup, thereby proving his point.

He was surprised by Pat's voice.

"How long have you been up?"

He turned to look. "You startled me."

"Sorry."

"Just got up. I'm looking for a coffee cup."

"On cabinet to your left. Where they've always been."

"What's your agenda for today?"

"Fully wake up. Then decide what to eat. That's as far as I've gotten."

"No leaps of the imagination for the esteemed Judge Knowles, eh?"

"The esteemed Judge Knowles leaps for no one." Pat did not have a quick laugh; her laugh was a vein of coal in a very deep mine, hard to excavate but worth the effort. Often, Jim wasn't sure whether or not she was intentionally or accidentally being wry; only after the fact could he tell. The sure sign was the way she had of glancing at him when she thought she had scored a point, of sidling up to him and veering away at the last moment, too dignified to say "ta da!" out loud.

Jim found a cup and poured himself coffee. The machine was on timer, so the coffee was ready and waiting. He wished life came that way.

Jim leaned against the counter. The coffee tasted acrid today; he wasn't sure why. Pat was rinsing strawberries to go with her granola.

"How did Connie and Crankshaft meet?" Jim asked, idly.

"A mutual friend introduced them."

"Let's say for a second that Crankshaft did in fact push Timothy off the trail and was worried speculation to that effect might reach social media. In that case, Crankshaft's career might follow Timothy off the cliff."

"Or not," Pat replied, "If danger is a real part of Crankshaft's image and he is accused of an actual murder, sales would probably skyrocket. I have no insight into how performers think, but my sense is they're willing to sacrifice everything for the sake of their careers."

"I agree, but a sleuth – amateur or pro – has to be ready to discard the obvious in favor of the obscure."

Pat pulled her chair close to the table. "I have no idea what you just said."

"Trust your gut is all I'm saying."

"My gut says to leave the case alone while I eat. By the way, I'm meeting Connie again. That she wants to meet with me so often is a sign of how troubled she is about being in danger, it seems to me. I'll let you know what she says. I'm meeting her in Harvard Square. I'll come to your place afterwards."

Jim walked home from Beacon Hill. It was a long walk but it gave him an excuse to walk Beauty Shop Row. The Row grounded Jim in reality even though it was devoted to artifice. He stopped on the way at The Long Gone.

Jim took his mug of house roast to an empty table and checked his watch. Pat and Connie were meeting at that hour. He wondered how long they would talk. .

He stalled at The Long Gone as long as he could, then walked the remaining half-mile home. His living room got good light in late afternoon, but not before. He carried yesterday's mail to his most comfortable chair and turned on the reading lamp. As was true most days, the mail consisted largely of catalogs. Given how little he ordered online, he wondered how his name had gotten on so many mailing lists.

The next thing he knew Pat was standing over him, looking down.

"When did you get here?" Jim asked.

"You were asleep."

"No, I was napping." Jim pushed himself up from the chair. "How did your meeting with Connie go?"

"Well. When you're awake, join me in the kitchen and I'll fill you in."

Jim did his best to jump to his feet. "I'm awake."

"Be careful. Don't fall."

Pat went to the kitchen. Jim took a deep breath before following her.

Pat was sitting at the kitchen table.

"Okay, tell me," Jim said.

"Sit down."

He sat. "I'm sitting. Now?"

"Connie sounds disillusioned. She's tired of deception as a way of life, tired of not being sure what's real and what's not. Is she in love with Andy or Crankshaft? She thinks she knows, then she doesn't. She's been unnerved about Crankshaft since the beginning, but since Timothy's death, she's flat out scared."

"Crankshaft is performing at the Night Shift all this week," Jim replied. "It's time for me to pay him another visit."

*

The Night Shift was to Ipsa Loquitur what the death sentence was to exoneration. Crankshaft's band had not started playing; the recorded beat was relentless. Jim watched the young people crowding the room. He wondered whether the beat they heard was as unyielding as the one he heard. If it was, did they like it or were they inured to it?

Standing at the bar, he was shocked to see his feet move ever so slightly. At least his head didn't bob, but my God! Was he starting to like the pile driver beat? The pounding swept Jim away and he was standing on a mountainside watching Crankshaft take two swift strides and shove Timothy off the trail. The vision was so real and the beat so relentless that Jim became worried about his mental stability. What was happening to him?

He didn't know whether he should share his unease with Pat because she could be impatient with things that lacked citation to a case or a source. She was reading in bed when he got home.

"Why are you still awake?"

"I was waiting to hear what you had learned from your pub crawling."

"I didn't crawl, I shuffled." He started to undress. "What did I learn? Not much. I just absorbed the atmosphere, which made me want to jump off a cliff."

"What's wrong, Jim?"

"Pat, do I still seem sane to you?"

"Always. Why?"

"Listen to a pile driver beat long enough and you start to doubt your grip on reality."

Pat absorbed that before giving Jim a gentle order, delivered without a gavel but an order nonetheless, "Come to bed."

He was surprised when he slept soundly. No dreams, at least none that he could remember the next morning.

Pat was getting dressed when he awoke.

"What time is it?" he asked from bed.

"6:20," she said.

"Why are you up so early?"

"I'm meeting Connie for breakfast."

"This early?"

"Eight o'clock. It was the only time she had and she wants to see me today. Are you awake?"

He sat up straight. "Yes."

"I'm going downstairs."

Pat started out of the room.

"Pat?"

"Yes?"

"Nothing."

"What were you about to say?"

"You'll catch me if I'm about to fall off a cliff, won't you?"

Pat turned. "What brought this on?"

"I need you more than ever."

"Did something last night bring this on?"

"Not just last night. You and I stuck to reality during our careers, but I've become unstuck and it scares me."

"Jim, you don't have to pursue this case any longer if it's bothering you. It's officially closed, remember?"

"It's personal now."

9

The bouncer at the Night Shift stopped Jim at the door. The noise coming from the bar was ear-shattering.

"You're the judge, aren't you?" the bouncer asked.

"I was, yes, Judge Randall, retired."

"Crankshaft wants to see you. Wait here."

Jim did as he was told. The bouncer ducked back inside. A moment later, he came out with meek Andy Taylor, which was a jolt when Jim was expecting Crankshaft.

"Hi, can we talk somewhere? I don't go on for 45 minutes."

"Where do you suggest we talk?"

"Come with me." Andy led Jim into a dark space behind the bar. The beat was still loud but Jim could hear himself think. What's going on? he thought. What is he going to tell me?

Andy ushered Jim into a makeshift dressing room behind the bar. Seeing himself reflected in a mirror with sweet-faced Andy Taylor while a killer beat pounded through the walls was definitely surreal.

Andy turned to face Jim. No makeup on his face, but menace in his voice. "I like you, Judge, but I want you to call off your manhunt and let me live my life in peace."

"Are you threatening me?" Jim asked, taken by surprise.

"I don't need to resort to threats. You're smart."

For some reason that angered Jim more than the menacing voice. "I don't know what Connie sees in you.

You don't need makeup to be a killer. You pushed Timothy
to his death because you believed he was poisoning Connie's
mind against you. Isn't that right? Isn't that why?"

"Well, well." Andy turned away. In the mirror Jim
could see the surprise in Andy's face. The surprise was
fleeting, quickly replaced by menace.

"Well, well," Andy repeated and grinned. The grin
was more menacing than any makeup. "The judge has a
temper. No, I didn't push him, and so what if I did? You
have no proof."

"Are you sure of that?"

The grin again, even more sinister this time. "Yes, I
am, and now I have to prepare to give my fans what they
want." Andy reached for one of the makeup jars on the
counter. "Are you going to stay for the show?"

"I've seen it often enough. It's not my kind of music, if
one can call it that."

"Miles Davis and John Coltrane. You told me. Too
tame for me. Goodbye, Judge. I'm sure we'll see each other
again. You strike me as someone who doesn't give up. Well,
neither do I."

Jim did not stay. As he reached his car, he heard the
beat begin, thankfully faint now. He wondered what the
neighbors who heard this every night thought.

He felt hopelessly out of his element. He had let Andy
get under his skin. If that wasn't a signal to retire for real
and for good, he didn't know what was. Why couldn't he?
What was stopping him? Pride? Fear of boredom? Here he
was, formerly distinguished Judge Jim Randall, standing
on a North Cambridge sidewalk in the middle of the night

after losing his cool with a guy named Crankshaft, about to go home to the always self-controlled Pat, who was handling retirement better than he.

He unlocked his car door and drove home.

"How was it?" Pat said from bed.

"Do you mind if I turn on a light?"

"Do you have to?"

He kept the light off. "Andy Taylor is not the meek and mild nerd he seems to be, he's as angry and mean as Crankshaft. In fact, Crankshaft may be truer to who he is than Andy Taylor."

"That's a little judgmental, isn't it?"

"Some performers adopt a stage personality that'll get them noticed, some adopt a stage personality that allows them to expose a side of their personalities they're too shy to show, some adopt a stage personality that reflects who they truly are. I believe Crankshaft does the latter for Andy."

"Could he kill?"

"If he had motive. Explore that possibility with Connie, get her to speak about what motivates Andy. Does she know? Does she care? Or did she fall blindly in love with him because he's everything she's not, and that's all she needs to know about him."

"I don't think she cares, I think she's relieved to be with a good guy who can so convincingly play a bad guy. The Hawkins family is as tightly locked as a bank vault, and she sees Crankshaft as the safe cracker who can help her break free."

*

Jim's Vermont house was a few miles north of Brattleboro, a small redbrick city in the southeast corner of the state. The city is a homage to the 1960's. The town scent is marijuana; hippies and the homeless vie for top billing on the streets. It has a good bookstore, several arts and craft stores, a tattoo parlor or two, coffee shops, and a free-flowing river.

Jim had come north because Crankshaft had a weeklong gig in Brattleboro following his stint at the Night Shift. The name of the Brattleboro bar where he and his band were playing was the Ball and Chain. Pat had stayed in Boston.

Crankshaft sounded different in Brattleboro than in Cambridge. He didn't have to compete with city noise, he could modulate his screams.

Jim said hello to Crankshaft when the band went on break.

Crankshaft's satanic makeup glistened with sweat. "What are you doing up here?"

"I have a house near here. I come often – to Vermont, that is, not this bar."

"What brought you this time?"

"I suppose I'm becoming a bit of a Crankshaft groupie."

"Bullshit. You're here because you don't know which is the real me and which isn't, and it's driving you nuts. Are you proud of that? The distinguished Judge Randall, obsessed with makeup and masks."

"That's an exaggeration."

Crankshaft carried on. "And you hope I killed Timothy so you can record another notch on your detective's belt, don't you? You're wasting your time, but, hey, it's your time, not to mention eardrums. Now I'm going backstage to prepare for the next round."

"I'll be gone before night's end, but you'll see me again. Connie deserves to know how her brother really died. The truth and nothing but."

Crankshaft glared at Jim. "I care about Connie more than you do. She *knows* what happened, her brother slipped and fell. An accident. Okay?"

"Would you be convinced if our roles were reversed?"

Crankshaft had turned away. He spun back. "That's the point, isn't it? You can't accept that Crankshaft isn't real and that I'm not capable of killing anyone. You want to prove me guilty to relieve your obsession, I want you to accept the truth that Timothy's fall was a horrible accident."

For a moment, neither Crankshaft nor Jim spoke. They stood silently at the bar like old friends who have no need to fill every minute with words. Abruptly, with a withering glance but not another word, Crankshaft disappeared backstage. Jim could almost hear him seething.

Jim left the Ball and Chain before the end of the set. Timing was everything when trying to trap a suspect in his own lies. Act like you know for certain what happened, wait, back off; try, try again. Let the suspect taste victory, then squeeze him harder. Again and again. Patience, not toughness, is the most valuable tool in the amateur detective's toolbox, and Jim had almost given away that advantage by showing his temper.

In earlier cases, he had been surprised how often suspects tripped up precisely when they think they've won the battle. Crankshaft had slipped up, he just didn't know it.

Jim went straight to bed when he got to his house. Jim's bedroom in Vermont was smaller than his Cambridge bedroom. Tonight it felt cramped. He wished he could talk to Pat, but it was too late to call her.

He awoke the next day to a glistening morning. The sun had already turned the Connecticut River gold. Later in the day it would turn the river into pewter. He gave a shake of his head at the routine glory of it; *routine glory*, arguably the best kind, too easily taken for granted. (He earlier had tucked away *A Good Time To Fail* as a possible title for the memoir he would never write; now he added *Routine Glory* to his list. He liked the sound of it.)

On previous visits to Brattleboro, Jim had made the acquaintance of the editor of the local paper, Mark Sandburg. Nice guy who lacked the snark of some newspaper people Jim knew (not Sasha Cohen). Sandburg had taken over after the previous editor, Phillip Rucker, was murdered. After breakfast, Jim went to see Sandburg at his office not far from the police station.

Sandburg stood when Jim entered his office. A good-sized man, hefty but not dominating.

He extended his hand. "Good to see you again, Judge." He gestured to a chair. "Please."

"I'll get to the point," Jim began. "I'm informally investigating the death of Timothy Hawkins who fell from a mountain trail in New Hampshire not long ago. Did you hear about it?"

Sandburg nodded. "Of course. We covered it. My reporter didn't get a whiff that it was suspicious."

"Officially it wasn't. Officially it was ruled an accident."

"But you are skeptical?"

"Pat Knowles – former Judge Pat Knowles – was the law school mentor of Timothy Hawkins' sister, Connie. We have concerns about Andy Taylor, Connie's boyfriend, who was hiking with Timothy when he fell. He performs under the name of Crankshaft."

"He's singing at the Ball and Chain this week."

"You know?"

"It's my job to know. In addition, the Ball and Chain has a shady reputation in this town."

"I'll be at my house up here for a few days. You have my number." Jim stood to go. "Oh, and according to Connie, her brother was a super-careful guy who wouldn't fall in his living room let alone from a mountain."

As Jim was about to walk out of the door, Sandburg asked, "You'll be up here for a week?"

"I don't have a time limit. A few days at least."

Sandburg nodded. "Okay. I'll be in touch if anything turns up."

The drive took less than ten minutes but by the time Jim had reached his house, he felt profoundly discouraged. He was getting nowhere fast but hey, the medical examiner had declared Timothy's death an accident. Nothing depends on you. Relax, enjoy Vermont.

His ridge top house provided solace and a view in contrast to his Cambridge townhouse which only provided solace.

He entered his house and immediately went to the long window. He couldn't remember a time when he didn't look out the living room window before he did anything else.

The glare of the midday sun had shoved the river deeper into its valley and hidden it under a veil of haze. If the Connecticut River could come and go, what could be counted on? Snap out of it, Judge. Enjoy retirement, enjoy Vermont.

He went into the kitchen unenthusiastically, lunch being his least favorite meal (breakfast was his favorite). Peanut butter and jelly sandwiches got tiresome, but he couldn't think of anything else, so that's what he made. Maybe tomorrow.

Stop tormenting yourself; back off. Wait until the sun passes peak. Trust that the river would re-emerge. It always had and at least for the rest of Jim's lifetime, would continue to. Stability was a pipe dream; only change could be counted on.

Hard to wait. But sometimes it was the best option. The hardest thing about solving crime was ascribing motive. Clues were easy to find; motives were much harder and more problematic. If Andy did push Timothy off the trail, was it because he had some sort of personal grudge against Timothy? Had it been a heat-of-the-moment thing after they argued? Had Andy thought that Timothy was turning Connie against him, as Jim had been assuming? And the broader question remained unanswered; who was the culprit Andy or Crankshaft? Maybe having a dual personality was the perfect alibi – 'I didn't do it, my alter ego did.'

He ate dinner by the living room window and watched as the last gasp of sunlight turned the riverbank gold. Inspired, he called Pat.

"Hi."

"Are you having a good time up there?"

"I'm watching the sun go down as I eat. I miss you."

"I miss you. Oh, I talked to Connie again. She called me upset that Timothy isn't being allowed to rest in peace. Apparently she's been called back to the DA's office after she thought the investigation was over. Do you know anything about this?"

"No, Ted hasn't said anything. My guess is he's wrapping up loose ends, and that Connie shouldn't worry."

"I agree, but she is jumpy. She wants to mourn in peace."

"Who can blame her?"

"Jim, you do some of your best thinking in Vermont. Has anything new come to you this trip?"

"I've been pondering motive. What would cause Andy to push Timothy to his death, if indeed he did."

"Go on."

"Maybe Timothy knew something about Andy that Andy didn't want Connie to know. Something that Andy had done in the past. Lame, huh?"

"My, my, and Jim comes up with another term he never uses – lame. Vermont has given you a second youth, Jim."

"To the contrary, I feel washed up, in need of being wrung out and hung up to dry."

"Get some sleep, Jim. I love you."

"Goodnight, Pat."

"Say it."

"What?"

"Say you love me."

"You are very pushy tonight."

"Say it."

"I love you, Pat. Okay?"

Pat chuckled. "Goodnight, Jim. Sleep well."

*

By now Jim could recite some of Crankshaft's lyrics from memory. Which horrified him since the lyrics invoked blood and mayhem. As he drove to the Ball and Chain on his final night in Vermont, one damn lyric wouldn't leave his head.

"Kneecap the bitch, castrate the pimp" was just the beginning. It got worse.

When Jim walked into the bar, the beat drove words out of his head, for which he was grateful. It was like being grateful for a jackhammer.

Crankshaft was in fine form. He prowled across the stage, he snarled, he preened. Not even a hint of mild-mannered Andy Taylor remained. By the end of the set, Crankshaft was drenched in sweat. To a lesser extent, so was Jim. Listening to Crankshaft was an act of aggression.

Jim approached the stage. "I know why you did it."

"Did what? Sang my guts out?"

"Killed Timothy. Where can we talk?"

"Who says I want to?" Crankshaft wiped his face with the towel that a crew member handed him.

"You're curious what I have to say aren't you?"

Crankshaft stepped down from the low stage. "No."

"Did you kill Timothy on your own or did Connie put you up to it?"

Crankshaft didn't flinch. "I told you, I didn't kill him, it was an accident." He headed backstage. "And you can go straight to hell."

"Rule number one in dealing with former judges, Andy: we don't quit. You should realize that by now."

"I realize you are one giant pain in the ass. What's in this for you?"

"A deep respect for the law, for seeing that the guilty don't go free."

They reached the door to backstage. Crankshaft paused a second. "You think you're better than me, don't you? You all do. Better than me." He pushed open the door. A whiff of sweaty backstage air hit Jim.

Jim replied while walking, "Actually, I think we're all made of the same stuff. Circumstances differ but not human nature."

"Do you hope that hounding me will get me to crack? I laugh at you. I have nothing to say I haven't said before." Andy gathered his thoughts. "But maybe we can put an end to this. So follow me."

Backstage at Ball and Chain resembled a hoarder's closet more than a dressing room. Crankshaft − visibly drained − sat on a folding chair and breathed deeply. "Playing a villain night after night isn't easy, let me tell you. No sir."

"Why do you do it?"

"Release. There were times on the bench you wanted to scream, right?"

"Many times, but I restrained myself. I'm guessing you put yourself through this night after night primarily because you love music, and performing is your way of selling the music. Your love of music came first. Is that right?"

Crankshaft looked surprised. "Are you a musician?"

Jim laughed. "Me? No, not a chance. My remaining question: have you become Crankshaft for real? If I wanted to off somebody, I'd adopt a persona that would be so extreme that no one could suspect it of being real. Is that what you have done?"

A twinkle briefly appeared in Crankshaft's eyes. "Good for you. The judge has an imagination." Two muted chuckles. "I'm enjoying this. Don't stop."

Jim warned himself: Don't let him get under your skin this time. Stay calm. "Connie deserves to know the truth about her brother's death. You were the only one there. What happened on that mountain? No bullshit. No performing. What happened?"

Andy stood. He gestured to Jim. "Stand up."

Jim hesitated.

"Don't be afraid. Do you want me to show you or not?"

Jim stood.

"Good. Now stand two or three feet in front of me."

Jim did as he was told. "This far?"

"A little farther. Okay, stop there. Timothy was that far in front of me. He was a careful hiker, not a risk taker. He liked mountains, but didn't like danger; he liked the outdoors but wasn't a thrill seeker. That's why I wasn't watching him closely, there was no reason to. The path was narrower than many, but not particularly dangerous. The view was amazing – all of New Hampshire and some of Maine spread out before us – I had the feeling of being on top of the world and I remember thinking this sure beats being Crankshaft. The thought made me laugh! I must have shut my eyes for a second in laughter. I opened my eyes when I heard a grunt. Timothy had fallen off the trail. Judge, I hadn't tried to stop him!" Andy choked back sobs. "The anger you see on stage is me yelling at myself: save your friend, save Timothy! Grab him, save your friend! But I'm always too late!" He sobbed uncontrollably. "Too fucking late!"

Jim was moved by Andy's grief. "Officially it was an accident," Jim heard himself say.

Andy was almost spitting. "How does anyone know who wasn't there? I was there, I know!"

"Perhaps we should drop this subject. You have to go on again soon."

Another musician entered the room. Jim thought he recognized the bassist.

The bassist saw Crankshaft's face contorted from fury and sobs, saw an older man talking to him. "Oops, sorry," he said and exited the room, leaving Jim and Crankshaft alone again.

Crankshaft managed to say, "Sorry you had to see this." He looked in the mirror. "Oh, shit, I've ruined my makeup and it's time to go back on stage."

Jim went out front to witness the second set. The crowd was restless but good natured.

Crankshaft varied his entrances night by night. For the second set, he ambled onto the stage, taking his time. Arch-villains could do what they pleased. Amble, trot, gallop; hop, skip and jump. Whatever. Tonight he ambled carrying a trident. As he approached the stage, Andy gave Jim a strange look, somewhere between anguish and apology. Then, mounting the top step in a single leap, Crankshaft burst on stage spitting fury. He raised the trident above his head and howled. The crowd howled back.

Repeated exposure had been necessary but Jim thought he finally understood: the howls were howls of affirmation. We're all freaks; or to be precise, we're not the freaks, *they're* the freaks. Catch on and you're one of us. Condemn and you're one of them.

Jim had no need to stay longer. He had learned what he needed to learn. He drove to his ridge-top house past the shopping center, the police station and a gas station, reaching his house in twenty minutes. The house was dark. He didn't turn on a light or look out the long window; he wanted to think without the interruption of sight.

He fell asleep in his living room chair and didn't wake up until 3 a.m. Too late to call Pat. He called her first thing in the morning.

"I was worried when you didn't call me."

"I fell asleep in the living room after I got back from watching Crankshaft. He and I had an interesting talk between sets. He broke down describing Timothy's plunge. I no longer know what to think. He's a convincing actor, but maybe he's not acting. How is Connie feeling about her brother's death now?"

"To think he died for no reason is very hard for her, but she refuses to think her boyfriend had anything to do with it. In my opinion, she's mentally shut down. I think it will take a miracle to pry open her mind. When are you coming home? I worry about you alone up there."

"Why? It's safer here than in Cambridge."

"You're seventy. Heart attacks happen to people your age, Jim."

"Heart attacks happen to younger people, too."

"I know they do, but there are more hospitals down here than up there."

"I'll be fine. Chasing crooks keeps me young. You know the standard medical advice for old folks: avoid excessive salt, get regular exercise, and chase criminals."

Pat gave a dignified groan, not too big, not too small.

"Pat, as you can tell I am doubting myself more than usual. Who is Crankshaft, is he all makeup and mask? What is reality? You should see him on stage. You'd be surprised as convincing his wildly improbable act is. Where is the dividing line between fantasy and reality?"

Pat tried to reassure Jim. "Because Crankshaft's whole persona is predicated on artifice, he's very good at it."

"But I pride myself on being a fair to middling sleuth."

"You're only human, Jim."

"I shouldn't be too hard on myself, you're saying?"

"Oh, no, be hard on yourself, be very hard on yourself. It's good for the soul once in awhile."

"From this far north, I can't tell when you're serious and when you're not."

"Come home, Jim. Come home to reality."

10

Jim drove home the next day. He stopped in Cambridge before going to Pat's. It felt good to be home. He knew where everything was, could walk through the house without bumping into anything. Could be young Jim Randall before he became Judge Randall, a young man with a good brain and no career goals. He had felt guilty about having no clear goals before he stumbled on the law. When he was first appointed to the Superior Court, he felt inadequate to judge others, but after twenty-one years on the bench, had become reasonably adept at it except for times like this when he couldn't make up his mind.

He turned on a single lamp in the living room before going to the kitchen and fixing himself a sandwich. Munching, he called Pat.

"I'm home," he said.

"Swallow, Jim. Finish chewing, then swallow."

He did as he was told, but not without bristling. "I know how to eat."

"Sometimes you get too distracted to swallow. You're home?"

"I am, and I'd like to come over. I've missed you, for reasons which at the moment escape me."

"I'll be here."

"I'll leave after I finish swallowing."

The Red Line to Charles Street was direct, which was about the only praise one could give it. The tracks between

Harvard Square and Kendall Square were out of alignment, so the trains had to crawl to avoid derailing, giving Jim ample time to observe other passengers – a mixture of Harvard and MIT types, tourists with guidebooks, high school kids with backpacks, men and women in business clothes, and the homeless. When the train picked up speed at Kendall, the relief in the car was palpable. Then the train climbed the Longfellow Bridge – the view of the Charles prying apart Boston and Cambridge always made Jim catch his breath – and down the other side of the bridge to Beacon Hill and Pat's.

Pat heard him unlocking her door and beat him to it.

"Hi, there. The house rule is no heavy metal fans allowed. I'll make an exception for you, you self-doubting fool. Come in, Jim."

He rolled his eyes. "May I sit, madam?"

"May I bring you something to drink?"

"Just sit. I want to be in the same room as you. We don't have to talk."

"What if I have something to say?"

"Zip it."

Pat laughed loudly. "Zip it? Is that what you said?"

Jim smiled. "Yes."

Pat's living room chairs were comfortable, unlike her kitchen chairs which were punishing. He wanted to confess his sins whenever he was in her kitchen.

"It's good to be back, but I'm less certain than ever about what happened to Timothy. I had hoped to provide Connie with certainty but I've lost whatever ability I had to distinguish the true from the false, accident from intention, Andy from Crankshaft."

"Jim, turn off your brain. It's bypassed the emergency shutoff and is spinning out of control."

"I think I'd like a glass of water."

Pat started to rise, but Jim stopped her. "I'll get it. You stay put. Want anything?"

"No."

Jim went into the kitchen and poured himself a glass of water. He drank it standing at the sink. Jim must have been at the sink longer than he realized because Pat came to check on him.

"Still alive?" she turned off the water which Jim had left running. "Are you okay?"

"Fine. Just thinking. Thinking at the sink." He chuckled at himself. "What now? I've let Connie down."

"You have not. Don't think like that."

"I hate to admit defeat."

"Not defeat, Jim. Accepting reality."

"What is reality? That is the question. I know, I know, get over myself."

Jim only woke once during the night, which proved to him how exhausted he had been. While awake, he became conscious of the traffic hum he had missed while in Vermont. Leave the pile driver beats to the young; it was traffic hum for him.

First thing in the morning, he texted Ted to suggest meeting after work. They met, as usual, at Ipsa Loquitur. The noise of lawyers venting was somewhere between traffic hum and Crankshaft at full scream.

Ted had a drink in hand when Jim arrived.

"Louder than Vermont."

Ted cupped his ear. "What?"

Jim raised his voice. "It's louder in here than usual."

"Big case went our way today. This is the sound of lawyers celebrating. What have you got for me?"

"Why do you think I have something?"

"Because I've known you for too many years to think you wanted to socialize. What's on your mind?"

"Timothy Hawkins's death in the White Mountains. You and I talked about the case before I went up to Vermont, remember?"

"It was ruled an accident."

"Yes. Hear me out. I just spent a few punishing evenings listening to his hiking companion – Andy Taylor, aka Crankshaft – at the Ball and Chain in Brattleboro. I cringe even saying the name Crankshaft."

Ted rested his hand on Jim's shoulder. "Pub-crawling at your age...shocking."

"Don't make fun of me. I may lack a gavel these days, but I'm a hale and hearty senior citizen, ready to rave. Be right back."

Jim went to the bar, shouted an order (the Ipsa Loquitur had decent red wine), and carried the wine back to where he had been talking to Ted, who was by now deep in conversation with a much younger man.

"Jim, this is Ned Olsen. He just joined our office after graduating from BU law school. Off to a good start. Ned, this is Judge Randall."

Young Olsen looked star struck. "*The* Judge Randall?"

"I used to be a judge, yes; now I'm trying to be a detective."

Ted said, "Don't be fooled by his faux-modesty. Jim is full to the brim with himself."

Jim touched his forehead. "Yep. Up to here." He shook Olsen's hand. "Nice to meet you. Good luck in your career."

"It's an honor, sir."

"Oh, please."

Ted said, "See? Faux-modesty."

Jim laid his hand on Ted's shoulder. "I may be full of myself but this man is full of it."

Ned Olsen laughed an appreciative junior-lawyer's laugh. "Nice to meet you, sir," he said to Jim.

When Olsen had left, Ted said, "He's one of the best of this year's crop, and he's in awe of you obviously, which I'll try not to hold against him."

"Ted, have you heard anything new about the death of Timothy Hawkins?"

"No, have you?"

"While I was in Vermont I went to see Andy Taylor/Crankshaft perform. Andy blames himself for not reaching out in time to stop Timothy from falling. I initially thought he was faking, but now I'm not so sure." Jim leaned closer to Ted. "Ted, I'm worried that I'm losing my sleuthing ability, such as it was. You'll tell me if you think that's true, won't you?"

"Seriously?"

"Yes."

"You and I give each other so much grief, I can't always tell when you're being serious. In answer to your question, I don't think you're losing your sleuthing ability. Of course, you never had that much to lose...See? I can't resist."

"That's all I need to know, thanks. If you hear anything new you'll let me know? Right?"

"Of course. Goes without saying. Are you leaving already?"

"I've become even more anti-social if that's possible. See you later."

When Jim got home he entered his house quietly for no reason since Pat was at her Beacon Hill apartment. He climbed the stairs to his study, wanting to be surrounded by books. He chose one of the few Simenon mysteries he hadn't read and sat down to read. Before he began, he looked out the window at the geometric rooftops of Cambridge (The Geometric Rooftops of Cambridge, sounds like the title of a musical). Inspector Maigret – Simenon's protagonist – never failed to solve the case he was working on. Why can't you, Jim?

You're comparing your skills to those of a fictional detective, you jerk. Inspector Maigret ran into lots of dead-ends, Jim reminded himself. His secret for going on? No secret, just go on, that was Maigret's lesson. Go on, and when you're done, keep going.

Jim didn't fall asleep in his chair, he made it down to his bedroom and fell asleep in his bed. He counted that as a triumph.

11

An email was waiting when Jim in the morning. Ernie Farrell, Jim's computer guru, "I may have something for you. The Long Gone this morning?"

Jim dressed hurriedly (made easier by the fact he wore the same thing every day) and walked as fast as he could to The Long Gone. The Long Gone did mostly takeout business in the early morning – office workers who wanted a coffee to carry to their offices, students with early classes, and amateur detectives hoping for a clue.

Ernie walked in, sat down and immediately began talking. "I discovered last night that Andy Taylor has a criminal record from thirteen years ago. Breaking and entering a pharmacy to get oxycodone."

"No kidding? Did he do time?"

"No, sentenced to rehab and community service. Since then his record is clean."

"I wonder why I didn't know."

"Andy Taylor used many names. He was convicted under the name Jerome Talbot."

"How did you happen to discover this?"

"I was researching oxycodone thefts for a pharmacy chain when I stumbled upon this. I immediately thought of you. Is it helpful?"

"Yes."

Ernie left as soon as he conveyed the news. Jim wondered how Connie would react to Ernie's news. Had she known about Andy's criminal record? How did Andy's criminal record bear on Timothy's death, if in fact it did?

He sat until his coffee got cold. By then The Long Gone was filling up with all-day laptoppers, changing the tenor of the place. Jim went to the counter to refill his coffee, then returned to his table.

Because Jim had gotten to the coffee house early, he was sitting where he could observe others while being lost in thought, his favorite occupation. The Long Gone was rapidly filling up and Jim would lose his space if he left the shop but his legs were telling him to walk, so he threw caution to the wind and left the coffee house.

The next decision was which way to walk. He wasn't ready to go home so the decision was easy – walk on Beauty Shop Row. Muse for the millionth time at how many beauty shops there were in close proximity to one another – and call Sasha Cohen while you are walking.

Sasha could meet Jim briefly at lunchtime, she said when he reached her. That would be soon so Jim didn't walk far. He turned back at Rosie's House of Beauty and beat Sasha to The Long Gone by a few minutes. Sasha was a good companion in addition to being an invaluable source. She buzzed with intensity, like high voltage wires or the hum of distant traffic. He had met with her often enough that he didn't always notice her intensity, but this time did.

"Hey," she said, joining him at a table near the rest room.

"Hey, yourself. Anything new on Timothy Hawkins death?"

"I was going to ask you the same thing. I know you were in Vermont at the same time as Crankshaft. I assume that wasn't a coincidence."

"How did you know?"

"Mark Sandburg, the editor of the paper up there, had read my reporting on the death of Timothy Hawkins and called me."

"Good for him."

A young woman entered the rest room, permitting an odor to escape that precluded talk. Sasha leaned back in her chair, oblivious to the odor.

"He told me Crankshaft is going on the road. Did you know that?"

"No, I didn't."

"Crankshaft is going on a five-city tour. First city is Providence."

"Conveniently timed," Jim commented.

"What's that supposed to mean?"

"Well, if a hiking companion of mine fell off a mountain and there's still some suspicion I pushed him, I might be glad for an excuse to get out of town."

"Cynic."

"I'd go on tour if our roles were reversed."

Sasha grimaced. "I'm trying to picture you fronting a heavy metal band. What would you call yourself?"

"The Imposters. My gimmick would be a gavel, which I would wield with wild abandon."

Sasha nodded gravely. "I can see it."

"Where do Crankshaft and his band go after Providence?"

"Cincinnati."

*

Providence, RI, was an hour's drive away. "I plan to drive down to see Crankshaft during his gig," Jim told Pat.

"You haven't had enough?"

"Come with me."

"Why?"

"To help me stay sane."

"Or you could choose not to go."

"I keep hoping to pick up a stray clue. Come with me, Pat, please."

*

Though not a long drive, the traffic between Boston and Providence makes the drive hard on the nerves. Jim controlled his frustration until Attleboro. "What the hell is society going to do when traffic overwhelms the roads?"

From the passenger seat, Pat calmly said, "We're almost there, Jim. You've done well so far. Don't lose it now."

"I mean it. What will happen then?"

The bar where Crankshaft was playing was the Devil's Cave. Half a dozen cars were parked in front.

"We'll fit right in, you wait and see." Jim put the car in park and got out, as did Pat.

The noise pummeled them as they neared the front door. More than a sound, it was a physical presence, a bully.

Jim turned to Pat. "Got your ear plugs?" The noise assaulted them as soon they walked through the door. Crankshaft was leaning over the edge of the stage, wailing, his words welded together in rage. The band thrashed as if fighting for its life. Desperation was the word that came to Jim's mind, five musicians desperate to avoid falling into an abyss only they saw and avoiding it the only way they knew how, by shredding their vocal cords.

Jim checked Pat. There was a stricken look to her face, as if her judicial temperament had been snatched from her.

"Bring your gavel?" he leaned closer.

"What?" she replied.

"Never mind."

The Devil's Cage had two rooms: a room where the bands played and a barroom. Jim gestured to Pat to follow him to the bar.

"Are you okay?" he asked Pat when they reached the comparative quiet of the bar.

"I won't know for sure until I can hear again. Such anger! What do kids today have to be so angry about?"

"It's an act, Pat. When I've talked to Crankshaft between sets, his demeanor seems closer to timid than demonic."

"Listening to his screams, I have no problem visualizing him shoving someone off a cliff."

Somehow they endured the set. Crankshaft invited them backstage on his break. Jim was used to the sight of Crankshaft up close, but Pat wasn't. Sitting next to him in the closet that served as a dressing room, she visibly recoiled.

Crankshaft noticed. "Don't be startled. I'm harmless."

"Seeing you perform is unsettling. You seem so convincingly evil."

Andy loved that. "Success!"

"I mean it. Evil."

Crankshaft became worried. "So both of you are after me? What have I done to deserve this?"

"Guilty conscience, Andy?" Jim said.

"Get out."

"So your answer is yes?"

Crankshaft turned to his mirror. "Get out. Both of you."

Jim and Pat didn't stay for more. As they walked to Jim's car, he asked,

"Do you want to grab a room somewhere so we don't have to drive back?"

"Are you tired? Do you want me to drive?"

"No, stopping for the night would be a change, that's all. I so rarely offer to change my routine, you ought to jump at the chance."

"That you have become a Crankshaft groupie is shocking enough, Jim. No, let's go home."

"I was hoping you'd say that."

"So why did you suggest staying down here?"

"Oh, I don't know. To be unpredictable."

They reached the car.

"Your place or mine?" Jim asked.

"Do I have to make all the decisions? Okay, your place."

They climbed in the car. Jim said, "He got to you too, didn't he? I've rarely seen you rattled. So now you can understand what happened to me."

"I hope the bastard's guilty. I don't want to think of him on the loose. He makes my skin crawl."

"Who? Andy or Crankshaft?"

"You're obsessed by the duality, aren't you? Single or double, either-or, it doesn't matter. They're one and the same to me."

They were silent until they reached Cambridge. Jim came to life as he pulled into his garage. "Good to be home."

"We were only gone a few hours."

"Was Timothy an outdoors person? Was hiking in the mountains a normal thing for him?"

Pat responded, "Connie described Timothy as a nervous Nellie who took pride in overcoming his fears."

They got out of Jim's car.

"By chance, did Timothy have a fear of heights?"

"Yes."

"I'm starting to get the picture."

"What do you mean?"

Jim unlocked his house door. "If Andy believed that Timothy was poisoning Connie's mind against him, he could have used Timothy's fear of heights to get rid of him."

"You think he planned Timothy's death?"

"Possibly. He strikes me as paranoid. Or maybe it was spur of the moment. They were tired from hiking, stopped to rest, argued, the argument got heated and Andy shoved Timothy off the cliff."

"I still think it was an accident," Pat said, "Connie may be too distraught to think straight, but she knew both her brother and Andy. I'll ask her which scenario she thinks is most plausible."

Pat called from Jim's living room. Connie answered on the second ring. "It's Pat Knowles, Connie. Judge Randall and I just got back from seeing Andy's band in Providence. On the way home, we speculated about Timothy's death. If it's not too painful, Jim Randall and I would like to run a couple of scenarios by you. Wait a minute, let me put you on speakerphone."

A moment later, Connie's voice: "Hello, Judge Randall."

"How are you, Connie?"

"Fine. Go ahead."

"As Pat just said, we saw Andy's band in Providence and on the drive home, tried several scenarios on for size. Was Timothy an experienced mountain hiker?"

"On the contrary, he was scared of heights."

"How did he deal with fears? Was your brother the kind of guy who considered fear to be challenge?"

"Very much so. Timothy refused to give in to his fears. He wasn't a daredevil but he pushed his limits. I can see him walking too close to the edge, losing his balance, tumbling."

"That's one of the scenarios we were considering. Another is that your boyfriend took advantage of Timothy's fear of heights to get him out of the picture."

"What do you mean? To kill him?"

"Do you think that's something Andy could contemplate?"

Connie's voice became shrill. "Andy planned Timothy's death, is that what you're suggesting?"

"It's one of the possibilities."

"No, it's not. And I deeply resent the suggestion."

The phone went dead.

After a moment, Jim muttered, "That went well."

"You were clumsy, Jim. She's too vulnerable."

"Now you tell me."

"I thought you knew better."

"Apparently Crankshaft has shaken me more than I realize. I'll keep that in mind."

12

"Okay, from what Connie said, she agrees with the official ruling," Pat said as they ate dinner in Jim's kitchen.

"I'd love some evidence."

"Really? What more do you need?"

"Proof."

"You'll never get it. How can there be evidence that the fall was an accident? Conversely how can there be evidence that Andy pushed Timothy?"

"Crankshaft is the key."

"Do you expect him to confess?"

"I never have expectations when I question a witness. I deal with what I find."

Pat looked askance at him. "Jim, it's me. Your former colleague. Your concubine. You don't have to explain your methods to me."

"My concubine? Did you say concubine?"

Pat smiled. "I did. Do you like that?"

"As applied to you? I'm trying to wrap my mind around you as concubine."

Pat rhetorically donned her judicial robe. "Would you prefer former colleague on the bench, never crack a smile Pat Knowles? Would you prefer that?"

"No. Stick with concubine. When Crankshaft gets back from his mini-tour, I'll talk to him one more time then be done with this whole damn case."

Jim could relax until Crankshaft got back; that is, if Jim was capable of relaxing, which he wasn't – stewing silently about the mistakes he had made, regretting missed opportunities, yes – he was good at those, but relaxing? He could fake relax, talk about relaxing convincingly but relax for real? Not likely. In the interim, Pat kept in touch with Connie who insisted that Andy was more likely to extend a helping hand than push someone over the edge.

Sleuthing was rarely a matter of incontrovertible truth, more often a weighing of the odds. Truth be told, a coin toss would get it right almost as often as shoe leather.

Out of ideas, he did something he rarely did – email a suspect. He got the address from Crankshaft's website. The email was brief: 'Hope the tour is going well. I look forward to talking with you when you get back to Boston.'

The not-too-subtle message: I'm not done with you yet.

Crankshaft swiftly replied: Can't wait. Nothing I like better than to waste time with a second-rate gumshoe.

Gumshoe...what was the derivation of that word? Jim would have to look it up. But not now, not when he was hard at work waiting for Crankshaft. His butt hurt from waiting.

In the morning, restless after Pat had gone back to her apartment, Jim took himself to The Long Gone where he could think with other silent people, which made procrastinating feel like a communal act.

The Long Gone was half-full this morning. He ordered a large coffee and sat down at one end of a long empty table. He felt better sitting there than alone at home.

But face it, he was the least communal person he knew. He enjoyed the company of others but not in preference to time alone. Which made the coffee shop a good fit. Alone with others. The definition of Jim Randall's preferred place in the world. A judge's bench, or a communal table at The Long Gone.

Pat and he ate dinner at her apartment on Beacon Hill that evening.

"Connie has noticed a change in Andy since he's been on the road."

"He hasn't been gone long."

"Which is why she noticed. She's talked to him every day while he's away. She says it's as if he's forgetting that Crankshaft is a fiction and it's creeping her out. I told her she shouldn't worry, that it's a result of Andy being on the road away from people and places that ground him. But her fears were not assuaged."

"That's what I like about you, Pat. No one else I know would use the word 'assuaged' in casual conversation."

Even eating dinner in her kitchen Pat looked magisterial. She would have made a good philosopher/king, to use Plato's characterization. Even so, Jim didn't try to stop her when she offered to wash the dishes.

Crankshaft's band was playing small venues on the road, which made no dent in the press. But Jim could follow the band's progress on its website. In Tulsa, the drummer got busted for cocaine and lacked the money for bail but crowd funding got him out of jail after one night.

Jim was comfortable with the life had carved for himself but reading about Crankshaft on the road wondered if he would have been happier living a wandering life. Jim had no musical talent so he wasn't envying Crankshaft in that regard, but to be untethered versus rooted in one spot ?

Jim was glad he had made the choices he had. A long marriage to Joyce, a successful and satisfying career, and now a union of equals, Pat and him.

Dammit, he was happy. He was. Happy, you hear me? And where's my gavel?

*

Crankshaft and band returned home three weeks later with no fanfare, which matched the fanfare of their departure. The day after their return, Jim was surprised to receive this text:

I want to talk. When and where?

Jim showed the text to Pat to get her reaction.
"Crankshaft wants to meet."
"Connie alerted me he might. But I don't know why."
"Only one way to find out."
Jim replied to Crankshaft:

The Long Gone in Inman Square. 9 am tomorrow

Crankshaft's reply:

9 am? You gotta be kidding. 4 pm.

Jim habitually faded in late afternoon. Took a nap if he was home. But anything for the sake of truth, justice, and the American way.

The lunchtime contingent at The Long Gone had cleared out by 4 pm and the evening crowd had yet to arrive in large numbers, so Jim could pick his table. He chose a side table, middle rear, below the high window which had never once been cleaned, as far as Jim could tell.

Jim arrived before Andy, which gave him time to wonder what would be the reaction of The Long Gone regulars if Andy arrived in full-Crankshaft. Total freakout? No, probably a quick glance, maybe a double take, then a return to their laptops and phones – The Long Gone was an ocean swell that absorbs everything in its path without ever crashing upon the shore.

Crankshaft arrived in civvies, indistinguishable from the regulars. He approached Jim like someone who would rather melt into the background than emote in front of an audience.

"Hello, good morning, afternoon, whatever it is." He gripped the back of a chair as if in danger of falling.

"Oh, for god's sake." Jim was in no mood to cater to overgrown children. "Sit down. You're making me nervous."

Andy/Crankshaft did as he was told. He sat and sighed. "I've been on the road."

"Andy, if you don't relax, I'm going to pink paper you."

Andy shook his head. "I don't know what that means."

"Have you involuntarily committed. You look as if you are coming unglued."

"The tour took a lot out of me."

"Do you want coffee? You have to go to the counter and order that."

Andy looked where Jim was pointing. "I'll pass." Andy sat.

"I followed your tour from afar. It went well?"

"I may not be cut out for this life much longer. It's the life I've craved since I was a teen, but I'm having second thoughts. I don't have any real musical talent, and I'm not sure I want to make screaming my career."

"That decision's in the future. What I'm interested in now is closing the case on Timothy Hawkins's death."

"I thought it was closed – it was ruled an accident." Andy didn't need makeup to be menacing. "And I'm tired of your suspicions. I *liked* Timothy, he was not only my chick's brother, he was a good guy." Andy paused, stammered, whispered with the intensity of a scream, "The silence when he fell! The *silence*! No cry for help! Utter and total silence! I don't care if you believe me, I know what happened! Thank God Crankshaft gets to scream on stage, or I'd go nuts. Okay? Is that what you wanted to hear?" He stopped talking and glanced at Jim with the bewildered expression of a child whose face has been scrubbed clean by a washcloth-wielding mother. "I didn't try to grab him, I didn't, I just watched him go over, just watched him go over." He moaned quietly. "Oh, God!"

How could Jim comfort a man who made his skin crawl? But he tried. "You probably couldn't have stopped him even if you had tried."

Andy had seemed oblivious to the other people in the coffee shop. He became sheepish. "Are we going to get kicked out? I'm really sorry to embarrass you, but sometimes you seem more like a priest than a judge."

Jim was mildly amused by that. "No one's ever said that about me before."

"A priest hearing confessions."

Jim gave a measured grin: "And when I was a judge I could put people in jail. Forgive their sins and send them to prison. One stop shopping."

A quiet burst of laughter broke through Andy's despair. "A full-service judge!" He stood. "I changed my mind about coffee. Be right back."

Jim watched him go. Every once in a while Jim became aware of his limits as an amateur detective. In such moments he wondered if his few successes were more a matter of dumb luck than brilliant sleuthing. Andy returned with coffee, a changed man, not confident but calm. "I apologize for embarrassing you. I'm surprised you didn't leave."

"Believe me, The Long Gone has seen worse. While you drink your coffee I want to hear how you came up with Crankshaft as an alter ego."

"I wanted something down and dirty. I ran through auto parts in my mind and settled on Crankshaft."

"Good explanation."

"What would be your stage name if judges had stage names?"

"Mine? Pat would howl with laughter at the thought of me with a stage name. Oh, I don't know, maybe Oil Change."

"You're okay, Judge Randall. A bit of a tight-ass, but okay."

*

"A bit of a tight-ass he called me." Jim laughed to see Pat's expression as he told her of the conversation at The Long Gone.

"Maybe leave off the modifier?" Pat said in reply.

Jim shook his head. "You're evil."

They were eating dinner in Pat's apartment. "You never know when I'm joking," she admonished.

"Au contraire, mon amour. I always know. I may not respond in kind, but I know."

"Since when did you start speaking French?"

"Andy has almost got me convinced."

"Wait, did we just change the subject?"

"Very perceptive. Yes, I swing back and forth between blaming Andy for Timothy's death and accepting the official verdict."

"And now?" Pat asked.

"I believe Andy's genuinely devastated by Timothy's death, which is not what you expect to see in a murderer."

"For what it's worth, Connie has never blamed Andy. She still doesn't. Shall we drop the subject?"

"I'm ready to concede defeat."

"My, my. Less of a tight-ass for sure."

*

"I remembered something," Pat said two evenings later at Duck, Duck, Goose. "I remember Connie telling me how troubled Andy had been early in their relationship."

Jim said, "Go on."

"When they met he was seriously depressed about his singing career, which was going nowhere. She initially wanted nothing to do with such a troubled man. But she was attracted to him – mainly because he seemed so needy – and before long they were living together."

"A fairly common scenario."

"Yes, but not many depressions spawn a Crankshaft."

"Depression spawned Crankshaft?"

"Yes. Andy found his muse and called it Crankshaft, and the three of them – Connie, Andy and his alter ego Crankshaft, lived together in an uneasy ménage à trois. Andy even wrote a love song for Connie – a love song in the key of Crankshaft: *I searched for the devil and found an angel.*"

Jim couldn't resist asking, "Would you like me better if I wrote you a song?"

Pat had a brief coughing fit. Recovering she continued, "Andy's mood swings scared Connie at first. She urged him to see a shrink but he refused, preferring to hide behind Crankshaft. She worried even as they talked of marriage and children. An untenable condition brought to a screeching halt by Timothy's death."

They were silent for a moment. Restaurant hum filled the blank spaces with sound.

"What was Andy's mood in the days leading up to Timothy's death?"

"Erratic. Manic."

And that was that until Andy fell to his death from the same trail that Timothy had fallen from.

*

The din at Ipsa Loquitur was louder than usual. Jim had to lean close to hear Ted – "The body was found by a hiker. Andy was wearing his Crankshaft disguise, which panicked the hiker at first. As far as we know, Andy was hiking alone. Jim, from what you knew of him, do you think his fall was an accident, or did he jump?"

"I don't know, but it could be a case of suicide by guilt. Raskolnikov redux."

"Citing Dostoevsky now, are we?"

"Don't make fun of me. Raskolnikov killed himself because he felt guilty for murdering a pawnbroker. Maybe Andy pushed Timothy to his death and couldn't live with his guilt, so he killed himself. The tipoff in my mind is that Andy jumped from the trail Timothy fell from."

*

Andy was buried, Ted's office closed the case, and Jim devoted himself to reading the newspapers and complaining. That is where matters stood until Connie found a handwritten note among Andy's scattered belongings. Apparently Andy had intended to give her the note before he died but had lost the note or changed his mind.

'Dear Connie, I know this will be hard to understand, but I am no longer willing to live within the confines of the law. I grew to think of the law as antithetical to human nature so I decided to become vengeance, to kill and die on my terms. To become Crankshaft for real, but I did not intend to kill Timothy. Connie, you are truly a good person who does not deserve further pain, but I could no longer let Timothy turn you against me. Don't tell me I'm nuts, I know he hated me. I only intended to clear the air, but on our mountain hike we argued about you and I lost my temper. He accused me of being bad for you, and I told him to mind his own fucking business and I pushed him. Connie, I shoved him! I didn't intend to kill him, I just wanted him to back off, but the next thing I knew he was falling, falling, falling without a word, silently, so silently. Connie, it was awful. I'm sorry I lost my temper, but temper is no excuse for what I did. I feel so guilty. I can't bring him back but I can even the score by jumping from the trail where he fell to his death. I can't expect you to understand. How can I when I don't understand? Try not to think badly of me, Connie. Goodbye.'

Jim and Pat didn't discuss the note until the next day, and when they did it turned out to be the last time they discussed it. Pat spoke first: "I spoke to Connie this morning. She was devastated by the note. Timothy *hadn't* been trying to turn her against Andy. Timothy died for no reason. I'm so angry at Andy. Jim, what would be your verdict if he were on trial in your courtroom? First degree murder? Second degree?"

"Probably second degree. Andy acknowledges he pushed Timothy, but claims he didn't intend to kill him. In my opinion, Andy may not have intended to kill him but was glad to have him out of the picture. It could be manslaughter, but I see it as a heat of the moment killing. No prior intent but intent at the moment of the murder. So I'd rule it second degree murder. How about you?"

Pat nodded. "I agree. Murder in the second degree."

Jim suddenly felt every one of his seventy years. "The law should have a category for killings that can only be explained by human fallibility."

"There already is. The insanity defense."

Jim shook his head. "Andy was sane enough to feel guilt for his actions. We need a new category to explain killings like this: sane but senseless."

*

Jim hasn't purposely listened to heavy metal since Andy died, but occasionally a pounding beat escaping the open windows of a passing car will pierce his chest and bring tears to his eyes.